In spite of that **no,** *Corrie was kissing him back.*

She was acting as if *no* was the last thing she was thinking.

He wanted to believe that. He wanted to believe her kiss and her curvy body moving against him, wanted to forget that a few moments ago she had told him to stop.

But in the end, he couldn't forget it. It was only right to make sure.

Yeah, he wanted her. Badly. But he knew that she had to admit she wanted him, too.

Somehow he made himself break the hungry kiss. "No?" he dared her. "Did you say no?"

She called him a very bad word, fisted her fingers into his hair and tried to yank his mouth down on hers again.

He winced as she pulled his hair, but he didn't give in. "Answer the question, Corrie."

She growled low in her throat and gave another yank. This time he let her pull him close. "Shut up," she said against his lips, and kissed him again.

Dear Reader,

It's that time of year again. The season of miracles, of light and joy. Of hope. And of family togetherness.

This Christmas, hardworking single mom Corrine Lonnigan is getting all of the above in the person of her former lover and now best friend, the father of her child, Matt Bravo.

Matt and Corrine had some rough times way back when. But they made it through. Now they're both leading contented, productive lives. They share the care of their beautiful five-year-old daughter. Matt has a girlfriend and Corrine has said yes to a wonderful man.

Everything's perfect. Until that fateful night in early November, a night that changes everything...

Suddenly the comfortable, easy life Corrine has enjoyed is no more. It's a Christmas of change, where risks will be taken and best friends become lovers all over again, a Christmas of second chances. This time around, Corrine swears she won't make the same mistakes again. But love has a way of challenging even the best-laid plans....

Happy holidays, everyone!

Yours always,

Christine Rimmer

R. A.

CHRISTMAS AT BRAVO RIDGE

CHRISTINE RIMMER

Silhouette®

SPECIAL EDITION®

Published by Silhouette Books

America's Publisher of Contemporary Romance

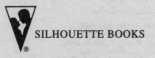 SILHOUETTE BOOKS

ISBN-13: 978-0-373-65494-9

CHRISTMAS AT BRAVO RIDGE

Copyright © 2009 by Christine Rimmer

Recycling programs
for this product may
not exist in your area.

CHRISTINE RIMMER

came to her profession the long way around. Before settling down to write about the magic of romance, she'd been everything from an actress to a salesclerk to a waitress. Now that she's finally found work that suits her perfectly, she insists she never had a problem keeping a job—she was merely gaining "life experience" for her future as a novelist. Christine is grateful not only for the joy she finds in writing, but for what waits when the day's work is through: a man she loves, who loves her right back, and the privilege of watching their children grow and change day to day. She lives with her family in Oklahoma. Visit Christine at www.christinerimmer.com.

For my mother,
whose loving spirit
uplifts and inspires.
Merry Christmas, Mom.

Chapter One

The doorbell rang at nine o'clock. Corrine knew it would be Matt, bringing Kira home from her regular weekend visit with him. He was right on time, as always.

"Come on in," Corrine called.

She heard his key turn in the lock. The front door opened and shut with a soft click. And then silence, except for the creak of a loose floorboard under his feet. The lack of happy chatter, of "Mommy, we're home!" told her that Kira must be asleep.

Matt stuck his head around the wall that marked off the entry, his straight brows drawing briefly together at the sight of Corrine on the couch, knees drawn up under her chin, ten half-full wine bottles arrayed on the coffee table in front of her. "She's conked out," he whispered.

Their daughter was draped over his shoulder, her

legs, in her favorite pair of pink footed pajamas, dangling loose. At Matt's whisper, Kira lifted her blond head, yawned hugely and then turned her face the other way, nuzzling against his neck with a contented little sigh.

"Carry her on up?" Corrine mouthed the words, gesturing at the stairway behind him.

Matt turned and went up. Corrine watched him go. Kira's little feet swayed gently with each step. Once he disappeared from sight, she settled her chin on her knees again and stared at the mess she really should start clearing up.

She was still sitting there, in the same position, when Matt came back down the stairs a few minutes later. He went straight to the fireplace and turned his back to the flames.

"Cold out there?" She gave him a lazy smile.

"Oh, yeah." It was supposed to get below freezing that night, rare for San Antonio in early November.

"Kira wake up when you put her to bed?"

"She didn't even open her eyes."

"Busy weekend?"

"The usual. Lessons on Saturday." Kira took tap and ballet, karate and modern dance. She went to kindergarten and day care at the best Montessori school in SA. These were just a few of the many benefits that came from having a rich, hardworking daddy and a mom who ran a successful business of her own. "We went to a movie Saturday night," he added. "Today, I took her out to the ranch." Bravo Ridge, his family's ranch, was a short ride north of SA, on the southwestern edge of the Hill Country.

Corrine lowered her knees to the side and tucked them in close. "Your mom still at the ranch?"

"Oh, yeah."

"How was she?"

He shrugged. "She seemed okay, but you know how she is, always trying to put the best face on things."

Corrine let out a small sigh of understanding. "So true…"

And then he did what she'd been waiting for him to do. He gestured at all those bottles on the coffee table. "And what the hell, Corrie? Pastor Bob know about this?" His tone was teasing, but she didn't miss the underlying note of disapproval.

She resisted the urge to say something snippy and settled for simply putting him in his place. "I'm not drunk, not even buzzed—and if I was, it's not like I'm driving anywhere. And don't you start picking on Bob. Bob's the best of the best. I'm lucky to have found him."

He tried to look innocent. "I wasn't picking on Bob."

"Yeah, you were."

"Uh-uh."

"Uh-huh."

He put up both hands, a gesture of surrender. "Okay, okay. I'll never say another damn word about Bob."

"Bob knows what I do for a living. He's not the least judgmental—unlike some people I could mention."

Matt huffed a little. "I'm not judgmental." Beneath the huffing, he was hurt. She could tell.

And she felt suddenly sorry. Matt Bravo was a great guy, really. A fine father, who doted on their little girl. And over the years, strangely enough, he'd practically become Corrine's best friend. She shouldn't be calling him judgmental—even if he sometimes was.

Time to change the subject. "Want some?" She tipped her head at the thicket of green bottles. "I've got plenty."

"Why not?" He was already shrugging out of his pricey leather coat.

She had half a tray of unused wineglasses. She grabbed one and chose a bottle at random, turning it to read the label. "A little merlot?"

He dropped into a wing chair across the coffee table from her. "Sounds good to me."

She poured, passed him the glass and then poured one for herself. "To our amazing, beautiful, brilliant daughter."

He leaned toward her so he could touch his glass to hers. Then he sat back. They both sipped. He gave a nod of approval. "Not bad."

"And the price is right."

He frowned at the tray of torn bread and the pitcher of water on another table nearby. "Wait. I get it. A wine tasting."

She nodded. "It went well, thank you. There were six of us, including me." She named off three of her employees and a couple of longtime friends from school. Then she raised her glass again. "I'm always looking for good values for the bar, and a few of these are pretty nice." Matt worked at BravoCorp, the family business. She worked in *her* family's business, too. Her bar, Armadillo Rose, was a San Antonio landmark. It had belonged to her mother before her and before that, to her grandmother.

Looking totally satisfied with himself, he settled deeper into the chair and sipped more wine.

"Just make yourself at home." She raised her glass again.

"I always do. Got anything to munch on around here—other than chunks of dry bread, I mean?"

"A few cold appetizers."

"Hand 'em over."

She passed him the tray.

He chose a cracker topped with sun-dried tomatoes and mozzarella and popped it in his mouth, reaching out to grab the tray before she could pull it away. "I'll keep that." He set the tray on the side table by his chair, grabbed two more crackers and ate them, watching her as he chewed.

With a distant smile, she turned her face to the fire and considered whether or not to bring up his mother a second time.

After a moment or two, he demanded, "What?"

She met his eyes again. "It's your mom. I'm worried about her. She came in the Rose last night."

He blinked. "Why?"

"She didn't say. She sat at the end of the bar and nursed a martini. For more than three hours."

He couldn't have looked more surprised if she'd bopped him on the head with the merlot bottle. "Three hours. You're kidding me."

"No." Armadillo Rose had live music on the weekends. Rock and hard country. It catered to a young, mostly blue-collar, party crowd. Aleta Bravo was in her mid-fifties, still slim and good-looking. She wore designer clothes and she had a certain air about her, one of money and privilege. Armadillo Rose just wasn't her kind of place. "She seemed…I don't know. Lost, I guess. I sat with her every time I could catch a few minutes. She told me how much she appreciated me and how much she loves Kira…."

He held out his glass for more wine. "My dad won't leave her alone," he said as she poured. "He's always showing up at the ranch, working every angle to get her to come back to him."

"She seemed…so sad last night."

His expression was almost tender. "You were keeping an eye on her."

"Of course."

"You're a good woman, Corrie." The look in his eyes had her throat clutching.

She glanced away. And then she felt silly and made herself face him again. "She, um, she didn't cry or anything. But the place was packed and loud and she would watch everyone dancing and having a good time with this expression that was trying so hard to be bright and happy but didn't quite make it."

"It's a tough time for her."

"Matt, your dad is not my favorite person. Still, it's so painfully obvious she's in love with him and always will be. I don't get why she doesn't just go back to him."

"Hey. Don't ask me. I don't get it either."

"It's been more than a month since she walked out on him." In late September, Aleta had left the big house in Olmos Park where she'd lived with Davis for as long as Corrine had known them. Matt's parents had always kept a suite at Bravo Ridge. Aleta was now staying there. Corrine shook her head. "And it's not like what he did all those years ago was news to her." Corrine and Matt had discussed this before. Matt had confided that his mother had already known about his father's affair. More than two decades ago, right after it happened, Davis had confessed everything.

Matt said, "But she *didn't* know that the woman he'd slept with was Luz Cabrera—or that there was a baby." The baby, now in her twenties, was named Elena. Matt and his siblings had learned they had a half-sister around the same time their mother left their father. And there was more.

A lot more. Matt's brother Luke had recently married Mercy Cabrera, who was Elena's adoptive sister. It was all beyond complicated. Especially when you added in the fact that Luz Cabrera just happened to be the wife of the Bravos' longtime sworn enemy, Javier Cabrera.

Corrine said, "I still don't get it. Your dad never knew that Luz had his kid, so why is he any more to blame now than he ever was?"

"But that's just it," Matt declared, as if that explained anything.

"*What's* it?"

"My dad *claims* Luz never told him about Elena. I don't think my mom believes him. And it was always a big deal between them, the whole total honesty thing."

Corrine poured herself more wine. "So you think maybe your dad actually knew the whole time that he had another daughter?"

"No, I don't think he did."

"But you're not sure?"

He ate another cracker. "I'm sure."

"Why?"

"Corrie, damn it. I just am."

"Okay, so. He busted himself all those years ago when he had the affair. At that time, they worked it out and your mom accepted that it was better if he didn't tell her who the woman was. *You* say you're sure your dad didn't know that Luz had had his kid."

He gave her a look. "And the point you're making is…?"

"That I still don't get it. It was more than twenty years ago. Your parents got past it then. Why won't your mom get past it and go back to him now?"

"She will. Eventually. We're all sure of that."

"All?"

"That's right. All. My dad. My brothers. Me. My sisters." Aleta had given Davis seven sons and two daughters.

Corrine asked softly, "What makes *all* of you so sure?"

"We just are."

"Please."

"Don't roll your eyes at me, Corrie. I know my own mother."

"I'm only saying, even given that she still loves him, it *is* possible that this time she's finally had it with him."

His brows drew together. "Had it? How?"

"Come on, Matt. You know what I mean. Maybe there's more going on here than we realize. Maybe she's fed up with him on more levels than just the affair he had so long ago. Maybe she's decided she's not going to take it anymore."

"Take it? Take what?"

"You know. Him. Your dad. The way he is, like he

thinks he runs the world or something. Maybe she's left him for good this time."

He gaped. "You mean divorce?"

"I do, yeah."

"Hell, no." He said it fast. Too fast.

"But, Matt—"

He put up a hand. "Uh-uh. No way—yeah, okay. They're living apart. Temporarily. But making it permanent? Never going to happen. Divorce is…not who they are. They're solid, married more than thirty years. They would never split up for good."

Although she thought he was in serious denial, Corrine resisted the urge to keep arguing the point. Really, what did she know about marriage and how a good one works? Her dad had abandoned her and her mother when Corrine was nine. Her mom had never remarried.

And Corrine herself had yet to take the plunge. Although she was about to, with Bob.

Bob…

Corrine smiled to herself. Sometimes she could hardly believe it was really happening. She was getting married at last. To a minister, of all people—a very special kind of minister. The kind who never judged or acted superior.

Bob's church, the New Life Unification Church, was open to people of all beliefs and faiths. Corrine, never much of a churchgoer before, had gone to New Life after her mom died in search of comfort mostly. A girlfriend had sworn she would love it there. And she had. Slowly, she'd gotten to know the pastor, never guessing at the time that Bob would turn out to be the man for her.

She glanced down at the diamond on her finger. It wasn't big or flashy. But it gave off a nice sparkle in the light from the fire. And Bob was such a good man, generous, sweet and true…

Matt shifted in his chair. She looked up into his gray eyes and they shared a smile.

"So what else you got here?" He gestured at the bottles between them.

"You'll end up drunk if you don't watch it."

"It'll do me good to loosen up a little." He held out his empty glass. "I'm a stick-up-the-ass corporate guy, remember?"

She winced. "Did I call you that?"

"To my face. More than once."

"I'm sorry."

"Forgiven. You know that. More wine."

"A modest little cabernet, maybe?"

"Pour."

Matt could have sat in that chair across from Corrie forever.

They tried more of the wines. A pinot noir and something Spanish. They talked and laughed. An hour went by.

Two.

Three…

Matt was having a good time. A great time—but then, except for a while there after she told him she was pregnant, he always did have a good time with Corrie. Sometimes lately, when he brought Kira home at the end of the weekend, he would find himself wishing he didn't have to leave.

Corrie's house was in an older neighborhood with lots of big, mature oaks. It had been her mom's house before Kathleen Lonnigan died and left it to her only daughter. It was nothing fancy, but it sure was comfortable, cheery and cozy, the furniture a little worn. Lived-in. In the past couple of years, since she lost her mom, Corrie had put her own stamp on it, things like fifties-style lamps and bright, geometrical-patterned rugs on the scuffed hardwood floors.

Tonight, with the fire going and too much wine making him feel all sentimental and pleasantly fuzzy, he kept thinking of that first night he met Corrie. It was almost six years ago now.

He'd been twenty-four. It was the night he came home from the University of Chicago with an MBA in finance. He went out clubbing to celebrate the milestone and ended up at Armadillo Rose, where he went crazy for the bartender. Until then, he'd never gone crazy over anyone. He wasn't the crazy type.

If he closed his eyes now, he could almost see her, the way she looked that night. Her blue eyes inviting him, that blond hair their daughter had inherited hanging over one eye. In painted-on jeans and a skimpy tube top that showed her navel ring. She'd danced on the bar that night. And he'd known he had to have her….

"Matt?"

"Um?"

"You falling asleep on me?"

He scrubbed his hands down his face, shook his head to clear the fuzziness and dragged himself up straighter in the chair. "What time is it?"

"After two."

"Impossible."

"But true."

"I should get going." He ordered his body to drag itself upright. But before he could actually make that happen, she got up and circled the coffee table to stand above him. He squinted up at her. "Huh?"

She leaned down and put her hands on his shoulders. Those blue eyes were so serious and she was frowning. "No way you're driving anywhere tonight." She captured his hand. "Come on. You can have the spare room."

He liked the feel of her hand in his and also the way the firelight made her hair shine like spun gold. "Naw."

She tugged on his fingers. "Get up, Matt."

"I'm fine here. Really. You go ahead to bed, I'll just sit here and…enjoy the fire."

"Uh-uh. I know you. You'll snooze for a while and then get up and go. It's not a good idea." She pulled on his hand some more. "Come on with me now. You can make it up the stairs."

"Acourse I can make it. The question is do I *want* to make it?"

"You're going." She spoke flatly, bracing her free hand on her hip.

He opened his mouth to tell her he wasn't. But then he shut it without a word. He could see that she'd made up her mind. Corrie's mind was one thing a man had no hope of changing. Not once it was made up anyway.

"Come on, I'll help you." She yanked on his hand for the third time.

"Corrie."

"What?"

"I'm a little high, yeah, but I'm not totally whacked. I can get up and walk up those stairs just fine on my own."

"Well, all right. Let's go."

He let her pull him up. Then, gently, he extricated his hand from her grip. "I'm going, all right?"

"So go."

He went. Halfway up the stairs, he realized she wasn't behind him. He glanced back. She was turning off the fireplace and switching out the lamps. He waited until she started coming up and then he went the rest of the way to the top and down the upstairs hall into the guest room, where she caught up with him. She flipped the switch by the door and the room became blindingly bright.

He blinked against the glare. "Ouch. Do we really need that light?" He aimed himself at the bed.

She grabbed his arm and pushed him down into a chair. "Stay there. I'll change the sheets." She started stripping the bed.

He considered the strangeness of that. The bed had been all made up, but she was taking it apart? "What're you doing?"

She shook the pillows out of their pillowcases. "Getting you fresh sheets. Bob stayed over last week and I never got around to changing them."

It took him about five seconds to process that, but his fuzzy mind finally picked up her meaning. "Hold on. Pastor Bob slept in *here?*"

She had the blankets off and the sheets gathered up in her arms by then. "Yeah. So?"

He frowned in thought. "But you and Bob...you're engaged."

Her mouth was kind of pinched up. "Is there a point that you're making?"

"Well, it's only...I mean, why wasn't he sleeping with *you?*"

She only looked at him. Her expression did not invite further comment.

He hit himself on the forehead with the heel of his hand and commented anyway. "Got it. You and Bob don't sleep together. Right?"

Again, she said nothing.

So he asked, "Why not?" He couldn't imagine being engaged to Corrie and not having sex with her. What would be the point?

Her chin hitched higher. "Not that it's any of your business, but if you *have* to know, Bob has certain principles."

"And by that you mean?"

She answered reluctantly. "We're waiting."

"Waiting." He pondered the word. "For...Moses to part the waters? For the second coming of..."

She shut him up with a look. Corrie had a talent with the looks. "If you know what's good for you, Matthew, you'll stop mocking what I have with Bob."

Okay, yeah. He was a little juiced. But he did know what was good for him and getting Corrie mad wasn't it. "Okey-dokey," he answered cheerfully. Then he slumped back in the chair, leaned his head against the wall and shut his eyes.

He heard her hustle off. A moment later, she was

back and bustling around over by the bed. He let his eyes drift open just as she bent to smooth the elastic on the bottom sheet. It was a great view. She had a beautiful, heart-shaped ass. And also this incredibly sexy tattoo of red roses and black vines that curled diagonally up out of her jeans from the left, across her lower back and halfway around the right side of her waist. From where he sat he could only see a section of it, between the top of her jeans and where her sweater rode up. He hadn't seen all of it in much too long….

Corrie had a sixth sense as to when a man was looking. Probably from dealing with an endless chain of horny, drunken fools at Armadillo Rose. She glanced back over her shoulder and caught him staring.

"Oops," he said with a slow grin.

"You are hopeless, you know that?"

"Yep. I am. Completely hopeless." He tried to look pitiful.

She fired the pillows and a pair of pillowcases at him. "Make yourself useful."

He put the pillowcases on the pillows. That took about a minute. Then he got up and went to help her tuck the blankets in—just to prove he was more than willing to do his share.

Not that she needed any help. With swift efficiency, she folded and tucked and smoothed. He ended up kind of following her around the bed, tucking what she'd already smoothed, kidding her by bumping against her—with his shoulder and then with his hip.

"Will you cut it out?" She snorted the words through a half-stifled laugh.

He bumped her again. She made a sharp noise in her throat and straightened to fold her arms across her middle. He straightened with her.

"What am I going to do about you?" She was trying really hard to look disgusted.

They were very close—nose to nose. He found he was getting kind of lost in her eyes. "Blue, deep blue," he heard himself murmur. "I've always loved your eyes. I'm glad Kira got them…."

"Cut it out, Matt." The words said one thing, but the softness of her lips and her breathless tone said another.

He had the wildest feeling that if he tried to kiss her, she just might let him. It was probably no more than a drunken delusion. They didn't kiss anymore, not ever, except for the occasional friends-only peck on the cheek.

And yet. As he looked in those jewel-blue eyes, he couldn't help thinking that she was thinking the same thing he was thinking.

A kiss. What would a kiss hurt?

Soon she would marry Bob Thompson, who actually was a decent guy, damn it, and the possibility of Matt's ever kissing her again—ever *really* kissing her—would diminish exponentially. Funny, but he hadn't thought about that until right now, half-blitzed in her spare room in the middle of the night, staring into those eyes that his daughter had inherited. Those beautiful, crystal-clear, sapphire-blue eyes….

Never to kiss Corrie again.

Uh-uh. It wasn't right. Wasn't possible.

Possible. Yeah. That was the word, wasn't it? That was

the thing, the simple possibility. She was not only getting married, she was taking away all the possibilities between them. Just wiping their slate clean. Bare. Empty.

What they were now—good friends, co-parents— that would be the extent of it. If it ever might have been more again, it never would.

"Matt?" She whispered his name. She sounded even more breathless than a moment ago.

He decided not to answer her. Not with words anyway. He only had to bend his head and his lips touched hers.

"Matt…" She said his name against his mouth. There was tenderness in the way she said it. And confusion. And heat, too.

He focused on the heat. He reached out and pulled her to him, wrapping his arms around her, turning the brushing kiss into something deeper.

Something hotter.

It was so good, the heat. The wanting. He'd missed it more than he'd realized. For way too many years.

She put her hands against his chest, pulled her mouth from his. "Matt. No."

No.

It was the word a man had zero right to ignore. But he did ignore it—at first. The bed was right there, freshly made, waiting for them. He took her down onto the softness. And he kissed her again, pressing her into the mattress, feeling the shape of her beneath him, so womanly and warm, so well-remembered.

And in spite of that "no," she was kissing him back, sucking his tongue into her mouth, pushing her hips against him, running her hands up under the sweater he wore. She was acting like *no* was the last thing she was thinking.

He wanted to believe that. He wanted to believe her kiss and her curvy body moving against him, wanted to forget that a few moments ago, she had told him to stop.

But in the end, he couldn't forget it. It was only right to make sure.

Yeah, he wanted her. Bad. But even half-plowed, he knew that her "no" couldn't be allowed to stand. She had to admit she wanted him, too.

Either that, or they had to stop.

Somehow, he made himself break the hungry kiss. He braced up on his hands and he stared down at her, with her blond hair wild around her pretty face, her mouth wet and red and so damn tempting.

"No?" He dared her. "Did you say no?"

She called him a very bad word, fisted her fingers up into his hair and tried to yank his mouth down on hers again.

He winced as she pulled his hair, but he didn't give in. "Answer the question, Corrie."

She growled low in her throat and gave another yank. That time he let her pull him close. "Shut up," she said against his lips and kissed him again.

He dragged his mouth away for the second time, caught her wrist, pinned them to the pillow on either side of her head. "Just say yes. Say yes or we can't—"

"Yes, all right? *Yes.*" She hissed the word.

"Well." He stared down at her, satisfied. And aroused, too. She felt just right beneath him. And he was so hard for her. Like a rock, despite drinking more wine than he should have. He bent, nuzzled her neck, muttered roughly against her throat, "That's good. That's perfect."

He raised his head again so he could watch her face as he pressed his hips hard against her. She moaned and lifted up, pressing back, showing him her willingness, her desire. Her sapphire eyes went to midnight, the softest, deepest kind of darkness.

She whispered his name. "Matt. Oh, Matt…"

The rest was like a dream he'd been waiting almost six years to have again.

They kissed. Endless, amazing kisses. They pulled at each others' clothes, unbuttoning, unzipping, pushing everything off.

And then they were naked. Her skin was hot silk. He rolled her under him and she wrapped her legs around him. He sank into her heat and sweetness.

It couldn't be happening.

But it was.

He was making love to Corrie. Again.

At last.

Chapter Two

Corrine couldn't believe it.

She could *not* believe what she'd just done. There was no excuse. Absolutely none.

She thought of Bob—his open smile, his trusting heart....

Oh, God, please, she prayed. Let this all be a dream. Let me not be a cheater.

But it was no dream. And she *was* a cheater. She had done it, betrayed Bob. Corrine shut her eyes tight. She wished she would never have to open them.

But then she couldn't keep them closed. She turned her head cautiously to look at Matt. He lay on his back. His eyes were shut. He seemed to be smiling.

Smiling.

He'd just helped her ruin her life—and he was smiling.

She breathed in deep and let it out slowly. She reminded herself that there was nothing to be gained by yelling at him, or by slapping that ridiculous smile right off his face. He'd only given her exactly what she'd asked for.

What he'd *made* her ask for...

A hot flush flowed up her cheeks as she remembered the way he had made her say yes. He hadn't even left her the comfort of blaming him. He'd made her admit she was willing. More than willing. He'd made her admit she wanted it. Bad.

"Matt." She spoke softly, her teeth firmly gritted.

He didn't answer, didn't turn his head her way, didn't even open his eyes.

She got up on an elbow and gave his shoulder a gentle shake. "Matt."

That was when he started snoring. A soft, contented sort of snore. And he was still smiling.

She watched in outrage as he turned to his side facing the far wall. He tugged the covers up under his chin with a happy little sigh. Oh, how she longed to shake him some more. And not gently this time. The least he could do was to stay awake and talk to her about the whopper of a mistake the two of them had just made.

But no. He was sleeping peacefully. And she was left to stew on her own.

She pushed back the blankets and jumped to her feet. He didn't move—and she hadn't left the bed all that carefully, either. She stood there naked, glaring down at him, thinking about how much she longed to wake him up and tell him what a total jerk he was for kissing her in the first place when he knew damn well that she was an engaged woman. And not only for kissing her, but for not simply stopping when she said no. For kissing her long and hard, until she was willing to say anything to get him to *keep* kissing her.

And then, most of all, for the rest of it. Which had been fabulous. Damn it.

Corrine put her hands to her burning cheeks. Somehow, that was the worst of it, that she had liked it so much. That she'd pulled him back down on top of her and started ripping off his clothes. That when he was inside her, she had sunk her teeth into his shoulder and cried out at how good it felt.

That she had come.

Twice.

No. She wasn't going to wake him up. If she did, she would definitely end up yelling at him. And that would wake Kira and that wouldn't be good.

So she scrambled around gathering up her clothes, which strangely had ended up flung into all four corners of the room. Her panties were out in the upstairs hall, for crying out loud. One of them must have thrown them there. The door was wide open, the overhead light still on.

God. Kira. She could have so easily gotten up and come down the hall and seen them. Corrine covered her face and whimpered in self-disgust at the very idea. But only for a moment. Whimpering, after all, wasn't going to do any good. She'd done what she'd done and now she was going to have to figure out what to do next.

She thought of her mom, her stomach knotting in

sadness and longing. Kathleen Lonnigan had been the soul of practicality. If she was there now, she'd probably say something like, *Well, baby. That was stupid. But time only moves forward and there's no one yet that can change the past. Right now, you just put one foot in front of the other. Keep moving forward and do what needs doing.*

So all right. It was one-foot-in-front-of-the-other time. She went and got the panties and put them on and then put on everything else. She turned off the light and closed the door quietly as she left the room. On tiptoe, she went down the hall and checked on Kira, who was sound asleep. The sight of that—of her daughter sleeping—made her feel marginally better. No kid who had just seen her parents naked could sleep so peacefully, smiling like a little angel.

Corrine went downstairs. She cleared away the mess from the wine-tasting party. By the time she finished that, it was after four. She trudged up the stairs again to her own room, shed her clothes for the second time that night, pulled on her favorite sleep shirt and dropped into bed. Lucky for her she was really, really tired. Too tired, even, to stare at the ceiling and think about how much she despised herself.

She rolled to her side, tucked her hands under her head and slept.

When she woke, it was daylight. Matt was standing over her, wearing the khaki trousers and wool sweater she'd ripped off of him the night before, looking worried. At least he was holding out her favorite mug and a delicious trail of coffee-scented steam was curling upward from it.

Corrine started to reach for the mug, but then she looked at the clock. It was nine forty-five. She let out a screech and threw back the covers.

"Relax." He steadied the mug with his free hand. "I gave her breakfast and took her to school."

She blinked. "You did?"

The worried look became a sheepish one. "I figured it was the least I could do."

"You're late for work."

"Yeah."

"You're never late for work."

He shrugged. "I called the office. They'll get along without me until lunch time."

Corrine flipped the covers back over her bare legs and plumped the pillows so she could lean against them. "Give me that coffee."

"You promise not to throw it in my face?"

"Don't tempt me. The coffee. Now." With care, he handed it over. "Thanks," she said grudgingly.

He backed up and sat in the chair in the corner. For a minute or two, they just stared at each other. He seemed to have no more idea of what to say than she did.

But in the end, he spoke first. "Look, as far as I'm concerned, it was the wine, that's all."

She wanted to believe him. She wanted that so badly. And hey, it probably was just the wine as far as he was concerned. Something he could blow off as lowered inhibitions and bad judgment.

For her, well, it was much worse. What they'd done

called everything into question. It made her a liar on too many levels. To Bob—and somehow even worse than that, to herself.

She sipped the coffee. "Yeah. A big mistake, all that wine."

He raked his fingers back through his spiky brown hair. "Stupid."

She sipped again. "Beyond dumb."

Another silence. Then he said, "And no one has to know about it. We can agree that it never happened."

Easy enough for him to say. He wasn't the one with an engagement ring on his finger. The closest he'd ever come to an engagement was his on-again, off-again relationship with Tabby Ellison, the daughter of one of Aleta's Phi Beta Something-or-Other girlfriends from college. Tabby was beautiful and rich and traveled in the same social circle as the Bravos. She would have made Matt a very suitable wife. If only Matt wanted to settle down.

But he didn't. Never had. Matt wasn't a ladykiller type or anything. He just didn't particularly want to get married. He wasn't ready for that, he said, seeming to mean that he would be. Eventually. Maybe that was true. And in four or five years, whenever that "right" time finally came around, he and Tabby would have a country club wedding and then Tabby would produce a couple of little darlings destined to grow up rich and very spoiled.

"Corrie, did you hear me?"

She puffed out her cheeks as she sighed. "Yeah. I heard you. And I can't do it. I can't pretend it didn't happen. Bob has to know."

"I was afraid you'd say that." He made a low, pained sound in his throat and rubbed at his temples.

She felt a certain...tenderness toward him. Okay, he'd started it last night. And he'd been more than happy to finish it after he got that yes out of her. Then he'd dropped off to sleep instead of staying awake so she could yell at him.

But this morning, he'd fed their daughter and driven her to school. And then he'd come in here to deal face-to-face with the mess they'd just made. He hadn't tried to slink away. She had to give him credit for that at least.

Softly, she offered, "There's aspirin in the kitchen cabinet, on top, to the right of the sink."

He let his hands drop. "I know, thanks."

"Did you take some?"

"I'm fine, damn it." He hung his head. He looked so forlorn, she could almost feel sorry for him—and did that make her a total sucker or what? She leaned back into the pillows and concentrated on getting more caffeine down. Several minutes passed. He slumped in the chair, looking at the floor, and she finished up the big mug of coffee. She was about to tell him they'd said all there was to say and he could go when he lifted his head and said, "I have to ask this."

What now? She set the mug on the night stand.

"I don't suppose you're on the pill or anything?"

On the pill...

Corrine's stomach did the strangest thing. It lurched, hard. As if the bottom had just dropped out of her world. She carefully smoothed the edge of the sheet over the blankets. Until he'd asked that question, she'd thought things couldn't get much worse.

Wrong.

She'd not only had sex with him when she was engaged to someone else, she'd had *unprotected* sex with him.

"Corrie, did you hear me?"

"Of course I heard you."

"Well?"

"No," she made herself admit. "I'm not on the pill. Or anything."

Matt said some swearwords. Several. "It's déjà vu all over again."

"What are you talking about?" She demanded, as if she didn't know.

"It's how you got pregnant with Kira."

She wanted to throw something at him, just for saying that out loud. "I'm not pregnant."

"How can you be sure? What about that Plan B thing they have now? Maybe you should—"

"Take my word for it. I don't need to load my body up with a bunch of hormones."

"Corrie…"

"It's the wrong time of the month, okay?" And, oh, she was so very glad about that. Her cycles had always been regular, her period right on time, every twenty-eight days. Her period had ended Saturday. Last time, with Kira, it *had* been the right time of the month. And there had been no Plan B back then. This time, there was nothing to worry about—except for how rotten, disloyal and irresponsible she'd been.

"You do seem certain." He looked relieved.

She nodded. Firmly. "I promise you, Matt. I'm not pregnant."

Armadillo Rose was closed Sundays and Mondays. But there were bills to pay, orders to make and deliveries to take. Corrine went to the bar at eleven that morning and stayed till three. While she worked, she kept seeing Bob's kind face, those soft brown eyes of his, his warm, generous smile that could light up a dark room, his gentle voice, the way he always knew to say just the right thing.

She called Matt on his cell before she left the Rose. "I kept Kira in day care today. Can you pick her up at five at the school? I would ask Sandra to do an extra night, but she's in Dallas visiting her mom until tomorrow." Sandra Yee sat with Kira four nights a week while Corrine worked and was usually willing to take an extra night now and then.

"No problem." He didn't even ask what was going on. He'd probably already guessed. "You want me to keep her overnight?"

"No. I'll come and get her later, by nine or so at the latest. If that's okay?"

"I'm on it. No worries."

No worries. She wished.

She started to call Bob next. But she stopped mid-dial. Barring some emergency, he would be in his office at home, beginning work on his message for next Sunday's services. She decided she would just go to him.

In no time, it seemed, she was pulling into his street

on the far west side, an area of starter homes not far from Lackland Air Force Base. She parked at the curb and went up the concrete walk, half hoping he wouldn't be home, that something might have come up to make him change his routine: a parishioner in need of counseling, an unexpected meeting of one committee or another. Which made her not only a cheater, but a coward as well, longing for any excuse to put off telling him what he needed to know.

But she got no reprieve. When she knocked, he answered, his face lighting up with a big smile of welcome. "Corrine. What a surprise."

She gulped. "If it's a bad time…"

"Are you kidding? I'm always happy to be interrupted by you. Especially today." Mondays were the worst for him, when he started on a new message for the next week.

"Having trouble with the sermon?"

"Yeah. I'm a little stuck, I confess. I get this feeling sometimes that I've already said all I have to say on a topic."

"You say that every week."

"And it's true every week."

"You'll think of something. You always do. Your sermons are wonderful."

He beamed. "How is it you always make me feel that I can do anything?"

She beamed back. Or she tried to. "What's the topic?"

"Sin and forgiveness."

She wanted to sink through the front step, just melt right down through the concrete all the way to the other side of the world. She babbled inanely, "Ah. Forgiveness. Well…"

"Come on in." He stepped back. Reluctantly, she moved forward. When he canted his face toward her for a kiss, she wanted to blurt it all out right then and there. But she said nothing, only brushed her lips against his, feeling like Judas at the Last Supper. Or maybe Cain stabbing Abel. He offered, "Want some coffee?"

"Uh, no. Thanks. I just, well, I needed to talk to you."

"Anytime. Always." He led her into the living room and sat next to her on the striped brown and tan couch. He took her hand between both of his. "Now. What's up?"

Gently, she pulled her hand free. "I…" God. Where to begin? How to tell this kind, gentle, trusting man that she'd gotten drunk last night and ended up in bed with Matt?

He touched her hair, one light stroke and then he pulled away. "Corrine. Are you all right?"

There was no use in stalling. It was cruel enough, what she'd done. This stuttering around over it was only compounding the awfulness.

She opened her mouth. "I…" And it came out all in a rush, one long ugly word. "IhadsexwithMattlastnight."

Bob said nothing. For the longest time he only stared at her, uncomprehending. Finally, he whispered, "No."

She bit her lip. Hard. And she nodded. "Yeah. I did. It was…" Excuses tumbled over themselves inside her head. *I was drunk. I didn't know what I was doing. I don't know how it happened…*

Corrine didn't say any of them. There *was* no excuse. She'd done wrong. Way wrong. Period.

Softly, he prompted, "It was what?"

She closed her eyes, shook her head. "All my fault. My…decision."

A long silence. At last he said, "I see."

She shook her head, hard. "No. No, I don't think you do. You're a wonderful man. A truly *good* man. You would never do something like that to me."

"Corrine…" His voice trailed off.

She watched his face, read his expression. He was trying to think of something gentle and wise to say. She spoke first. "It's not going to work with us, is it, Bob? We're not right for each other. You need a nicer girl than I'll ever be. And I need…oh, I'm not sure. But if what I needed was you, I would never have done what I did. I'm only sorry I couldn't have figured all this out in a more…dignified way." She took off her engagement ring and set it on the coffee table. And then she left.

He didn't try to stop her.

Outside, she got in her car and just sat for a while, staring blindly out the windshield at the pale blue sky. When she finally got around to starting up the engine and driving away, the dashboard clock said ten after four. She could have called Matt and told him he was off the hook, that she would pick up Kira after all.

But she didn't. She went home and made tea. Her mom had always loved a hot cup of tea. Earl Grey had been her mom's favorite, so Corrine had Earl Grey. She drizzled honey into it, just like Kathleen would have done. And then she sipped it slowly, staring at Kira's stick-figure drawings taped to the refrigerator, thinking of all the lovely single women at New Life Unification Church who would now get their chance at nice Pastor Bob.

It was the right thing to do, baby.

"I know it was, Mom."

You'll get over it.

Corrine held out her left hand, fingers spread, and stared at her empty ring finger. "I feel totally disgusted with myself. Worst of all, though, I feel relieved."

Almost, she could hear her mother's husky laughter. But only faintly, from far, far away.

Corrine showed up at Matt's large, pricey house in Alamo Heights at a little after seven.

"You okay?" he asked at the front door.

She had time for a nod and a tight smile before Kira came flying in from the other room. "Mommy, where have you been?"

"Busy, very busy." Corrine swung her up into her arms. "Big hug?"

"Yes!" Kira wrapped her arms around Corrine's neck and squeezed. Corrine squeezed back, reveling in the bubble gum and baby powder scent of her skin and the warmth of her little body so close. But her daughter's hugs never lasted long enough. Kira craned back, small hands on Corrine's shoulders. "Daddy gave me s'ghetti."

"Yum." She smoothed Kira's straight blond hair, kissed her silky cheek.

"Are we going home now?"

Corrine let her slide to the floor. "Yes, we are." She

flashed a falsely bright smile in Matt's direction. "Thanks a bunch."

He looked back at her steadily. "I'll call you."

"Unnecessary. Really. Kira, honey. Get your pack and your coat." Kira skipped off toward the living room, leaving her alone with him again. "Hurry now!" She called.

Matt said, "Where's your engagement ring?"

Corrine resisted the urge to whip her hand out of sight. "I gave it back."

He looked kind of stricken. She took more satisfaction than she should have from that. Before he could come up with anything else to say, Kira bounced back in, her Ariel pack sliding down one arm and her white quilted coat with the pink fake-fur accents dragging the floor.

"Put on that coat," Matt said gruffly.

Kira dimpled up at him as she dropped the pack and stuck her arms in the sleeves. "I *am,* Daddy." Corrine bent to zip her up, but Kira pushed her hands away. "Mommy. I can do it myself."

"Well, all right." Corrine stood back and made herself wait as Kira's inexperienced little fingers fiddled with the zipper base, trying to get the tab into the placket. She purposely kept herself from glancing Matt's way for fear of the look she would see on his face.

A guilty look. A damn-it-Corrie-I'm-so-sorry look.

"See." Kira zipped up and held her arms wide. "I did it myself."

"Good job. Let's go."

"'Kay. Bye, Daddy." She reached up her arms. He knelt and she hugged him and planted a big smacker right on his cheek. "I love you."

"Love you, too, sweetheart."

And at last, Corrine turned and opened the door again. Kira slid around her and raced for the car, backpack bobbing.

At home, there was bath time and story time and then Corrine tucked her daughter in, kissed her cheek and turned off the light as she left the room.

She'd barely made it downstairs when the phone started ringing. A glance at the display told her what she already knew: *Matt.* She let the machine get it.

"Come on, Corrie. Pick up….I know you're there and *you* know you need a friend to talk to. Corrie. Damn it. Corrie, come on."

Corrine left the kitchen as he hung up. The dial tone buzzed briefly before the machine clicked itself off. She went to the living room, turned on the fire and grabbed the remote.

Half an hour later, as she was watching a *That '70s Show* rerun and slowly drifting off to sleep, the doorbell rang. She sat up, grabbed the remote and punched the off button.

What was the matter with that man? Hadn't she made it crystal clear that she didn't want to talk about it, especially not with him?

She got up and stomped to the door in her stocking feet. As she disengaged the security lock and yanked it wide, she opened her mouth to tell him in no uncertain terms that she really, truly did not want to talk about it and would he please just go home.

But it wasn't Matt after all.

Corrine snapped her mouth shut without uttering a single word.

Aleta Bravo stood on her front step, wearing a silver-gray cashmere coat over what appeared to be a lacy black negligee. She had black satin bedroom slippers on her feet, a designer bag over one arm. And a suitcase flanking her on either side.

"I'm so sorry, Corrine. I didn't know where else to go."

Chapter Three

Corrine offered tea and cookies. They sat by the fire sipping tea and munching on Oreos.

Aleta spotted her ring finger. "Where's your engagement ring?"

Corrine shook her head and grabbed a second Oreo. "It wasn't working out." She opened the cookie, licked the white filling. "I had to, um, return it."

"Oh, Corrine…"

"It's…for the best. I mean that. Sometimes, well, it's just better that you figure out *before* the wedding that it's not a match made in heaven, after all."

"You're all right, then?"

"I'm doing fine. Honestly."

"Well, I'm glad to hear it. How do you kids say it? 'It's all good?'"

"That's it. Now, tell me what's happening with you."

Aleta's shoulders drooped. "With me, it's *not* all good."

"What can I do? Anything, seriously."

"If I could stay here with you just for a week or two…" Matt's mom stirred sugar into her tea. "I can't take it at the ranch anymore."

"Why not? What's happened?"

Aleta's gaze slid away. She stared into the fire. "Well, you know Davis…."

Corrine did know. "He wants you to come back to him."

"Worse. He *demands* it. You know how he is. He thinks it's perfectly all right to burst in on me at any time of the day or night and insist that I see reason—meaning that I do things his way. When I refuse, he gets mad. When that doesn't work, he pleads with me to give him another chance. Somehow, that's the hardest. Seeing a proud man beg…" Her mouth quivered and her eyes spoke of heartbreak.

Corrine said softly, "I'm so sorry, Aleta."

Matt's mom smiled, a smile without joy. Or humor. "Tonight, I was just getting ready for bed when he barged into the suite without even bothering to knock and started in on me about how ridiculous I was being, how I was coming home with him, right then, and he wasn't taking no for an answer." She looked down at her hand and realized she was still holding the spoon she'd used to stir her tea. Setting it carefully in the saucer, she picked up the cup and took a sip. "He's been doing that at least twice a week since I left him." The cup rattled against the saucer as she set it back down. "It's very upsetting."

"I can imagine."

"And not only to me. Did you know that Mercy is expecting?"

"Yes. Matt told me." When Mercy married Luke, the third-born son in the Bravo family, she'd moved in with him at Bravo Ridge. Luke was the family rancher. He ran Bravo Ridge.

"Mercy's just entering her second trimester. I'm very fond of her, you know?" At Corrine's nod, Aleta continued, "It's not good, though, all that yelling and arguing and disruption. Not for any of us—and especially not for a mother-to-be. So that's another reason I couldn't stay at the ranch. Poor Mercy deserves a little peace and quiet."

"You're right, of course."

"I'm just…" Aleta picked up her cup again. She took another sip. "Oh, Corrine, I'm at the end of my rope with that man."

Corrine sympathized. Totally. Davis Bravo was a rich, overbearing, fat-headed snob. Corrine had never liked him. And he didn't care much for her, either. He'd always thought his son was too good for her and he resented that she'd gotten pregnant with Matt's child. Over the years, Davis had developed something of a soft spot for Kira, at least. But he always seemed to look down on Corrine for owning a bar, for having a baby without getting married first—not that he wanted her and Matt to get married. No way. He had bigger plans for his fourth son than to marry "some damn slutty barmaid," as he'd called her to her face once way back when. He wanted Matt to settle down with Tabby

Ellison, who wasn't the least slutty and whose dad was almost as rich as Davis.

Aleta brushed a tear from her cheek and smoothed her negligee over her knees. "It's just so stressful."

"It's okay, truly. I understand."

"I've told him I need time. He won't listen. I considered a hotel, but he's shameless. He would have no compunction about bribing the staff so they would let him into my rooms. Here at your house, well, he doesn't have a key. And I know how you are." She smiled tenderly through her tears. "Tough and strong and self-reliant. He'll never get through you."

Tough and strong and self-reliant. It felt good, to know that Matt's mom thought so highly of her, especially after last night, when she'd behaved exactly like the slut Davis had once accused her of being. She smiled. "Well, your husband's a pretty tough guy. If he shows up here, I can't guarantee I'll be able to take him down."

For the first time that night, Aleta actually chuckled. But the laugh quickly faded. "If he shows up here, I promise to deal with him. I do fight my own battles."

"Whew. Good to know."

"I confess, there are several reasons I would like to stay here. It's so homey here. Much better than a hotel." Aleta glanced longingly around the fire-lit room. "I could be with you and my granddaughter. I could…help out. Watch Kira in the evenings, while you're working…"

Corinne didn't need to ask why Aleta couldn't stay with one of her daughters. Abilene and Zoe were in their early twenties and just getting started in life, living in small apartments not suited to an open-ended visit from their mom. And those high-class girlfriends Aleta had known all her life? Staying with one of them would be awkward, to say the least. They probably didn't even know that Aleta and Davis were living apart.

But Aleta trusted Corrine, felt comfortable with her. Plus, there was Kira. Aleta loved her granddaughter and jumped at any chance to spend time with her.

"Finish your tea," Corrine said, rising. "And have an Oreo or two. I'll go make up the bed in the spare room." She blinked away a sudden, vivid image of her and Matt rolling naked on that very bed the night before. "You're always welcome here, Aleta. Anytime. For as long as you want to stay."

Matt called again about an hour later after Corinne and Aleta were in bed. Corrine let the machine downstairs take it. She deleted it in the morning, unheard.

Tuesday afternoon, while Aleta was out at the ranch picking up a few other things she needed, he called for the third time. Corrine refused to answer. What more was there to say? They'd blown it royally. And they wouldn't be blowing it again. End of story.

Matt had barely finished leaving his message demanding that she call him when the phone started ringing again. That time it was Sandra Yee, Kira's nighttime sitter, with the news that she'd hooked up with an old boyfriend and decided to stay in Dallas.

When Aleta got home, Corrine told her the problem.

Aleta shrugged. "It's not a problem in the least. As I told you, I'm more than pleased to take care of Kira."

She also took over the grocery shopping—and the

cooking. Who knew that Matt's mom could cook? Aleta had always had help around the house, people who cleaned and bought the groceries and prepared fancy meals.

"But I would cook, too, sometimes," she told Corrine. "I enjoy cooking. I find it soothing."

"Keep it up. Please," Corrine answered, loading her plate with perfectly roasted lamb and new potatoes before heading to the Rose Wednesday night. "This is delicious."

Thursday went by without anything much happening. Matt didn't call. Bob had never called. By then, Corinne felt certain he wouldn't, which was for the best. Davis hadn't come around. Apparently, he was leaving Aleta alone for a change.

Or so Corrine assumed until Friday morning at breakfast, when Kira said, "Grandpa came to see me last night. He was mad but he gave me a big hug and then Grandma told him to go away."

Aleta and Corrine shared a look. Aleta said, "Sweetheart, drink your juice."

Kira frowned. "You mean you don't want me to talk about Grandpa?"

Corrine said, "Your grandpa loves you very much."

"But why was he so mad?"

"It's too complicated to explain, honey," Corrine told her. "All you really need to know is he isn't mad at you."

"He's not?"

Aleta reached across and stroked Kira's hair. "No way."

Kira seemed to be satisfied with that. She finished up her breakfast and Corrine took her to school.

Once Corrine got back home, Aleta offered tea and the orange nut bread she'd baked the day before. They sat at the kitchen table and Aleta talked about Davis.

She didn't say anything new exactly. Most of it was stuff Matt had already told Corrine, such as that Davis swore he never knew that Luz had had his child. "But I've known that man for a very long time. He would have felt some…responsibility for Luz, after what happened between them."

"You think he would have checked on her, would have known she was pregnant after their affair?"

Aleta nodded. "And he would have added up the months."

Corrine suggested, "Maybe he didn't want to know."

Aleta shrugged. "Well. I suppose that's possible."

"You're hurt that he betrayed you. Still hurt, even after all these years."

"I am. And deeply humiliated. I don't think I really forgave him, when it happened. I just decided to go on. We had all nine of the children by then, all of them under ten. Zoe was a just a baby and Abilene was still in diapers. I asked him to leave when he told me. We were separated for a couple of weeks. But I couldn't even consider divorcing him then. It seemed too wrong. For the children's sake. For the family. So we reconciled. I thought I was over it. But now that I know the woman was Luz Cabrera, of all people, and that she had Davis's child…"

"You mean you never *really* got over that he betrayed you?"

"No. I didn't. I see that now."

Corrine thought of poor Bob. Yes, she was still furious at herself for what she'd done. But at least they hadn't gotten married—let alone had a baby. Or nine. How terrible, to be betrayed by the one person who had sworn to stick by you, to be true to you, no matter what.

She suggested, "I know this may sound strange, but what about Luz? Maybe you could talk to her? Ask her if Davis knew that Elena was his." The idea wasn't that far-fetched. Luz, whose husband had left her when he learned of her betrayal with Davis, was part of the Bravo family now, as bizarre as that seemed. Not only was Davis her natural daughter's real father, but her adopted daughter, Mercy, had married Luke.

Aleta stared down at her untouched slice of orange nut bread. "Mercy says Luz told her that Davis didn't know."

"Well, see, then?"

Aleta only shook her head. "It's all just too tangled up and awful."

"You don't believe Mercy?"

"I think she's telling the truth as she knows it. And maybe it *would* be a good thing for me, to hear what Luz has to say. But frankly, I can't bear the idea of talking to Luz. I don't know how she would react if I approached her. I don't know how *I* would react, to find myself hashing it all out again with my husband's former lover, face-to-face. The last thing I want is to stir up more trouble. We have plenty of that now already."

Right then, the phone rang. When Corrine ignored it, Aleta sent her a questioning look. The machine clicked on. "Damn it, Corrie." Matt's deep voice filled the room. "Call me." Click. Dial tone.

Aleta arched a brow.

Corrine shook her head. "Please. Don't even ask."

Matt felt like a complete jerk. Probably because he *was* a complete jerk, pushing Corrie to have sex with him when she had another guy's ring on her finger.

But still. Why couldn't she take a little pity on him and return his calls, talk it out with him, give him a chance to be supportive over whatever had happened with her and Pastor Bob? It wasn't like she wouldn't have to deal with him eventually. They had a kid together, for crying out loud. A kid he took care of every weekend.

By 9:30 a.m. Saturday, when she still hadn't called, he knew she would be showing up at ten as usual with Kira. Good. He'd have another chance to get through to her, to get her to see that they couldn't go on like this.

He even had a plan. He'd bought WALL-E on Blu-ray. Kira loved WALL-E. He had it all loaded up and ready to go on the 65-inch flatscreen in the media room. Kira knew how to push Play. All he had to do was hand her the remote and point her toward the media room, simultaneously positioning himself between Corrie and the door.

It could work. And he was just desperate enough to get through to Corrie that he was standing in the foyer, remote in hand, when the doorbell rang at ten on the dot. Corrie had a key, just as he had one to her place, but they were both careful to respect each other's privacy.

He pulled the door wide, ready with a big, friendly smile—a smile that never quite took form. It wasn't Corrie who stood there with Kira.

"Hi, Daddy."

"Hi, sweetheart. Hey, Mom."

"Matthew." His mother put her slim hand on his shoulder and went on tiptoe to kiss his cheek.

He stepped back. As they crossed the threshold, he asked in a voice he made as casual as possible, "Where's Corrie?"

His mother's smile was much too sweet. "I thought she might enjoy sleeping in late. She works until all hours most nights, you know."

"Daddy, what's the 'mote for?"

Matt bent down to her. "Do I get a kiss?"

Kira took his face between her two soft little-girl hands and kissed him—a quick, hard press of her small lips to his. "There. What about the 'mote?"

He handed it to her. "It's all ready in the media room. Just push Play."

"What *is* it?"

"Go see." With a happy giggle, Kira headed off down the hall. A moment later, after a childish shout of delighted surprise, the movie started. Matt stood from his crouch. "Dad mentioned you were staying at Corrie's. He's not real pleased about it."

His mother's serene expression didn't waver. "Corrine has been lovely. I can't tell you how refreshing it is to be able to sleep through the night and not worry that I'll wake up to find your father standing over my bed."

Matt grunted. "Dad is persistent, if nothing else."

"Persistent is not the word I would have used."

"He loves you, Mom."

"Stay out of it, Matthew."

At that exact moment, he had a brilliant idea. "I wonder. Could you do me a favor?"

His mother frowned slightly at the sudden shift in the conversation. But she'd always been the kind of mom who was happy to help out. "Of course. What?"

He tipped his head in the direction Kira had gone. "I hate to drag her away from that, now that I've let her start it. But I just realized I need to run back to the office…"

She looked doubtful. "The office?"

"I'll be an hour or so. Maybe a little longer if I need to do some…research."

"Research? On what?"

"Long story. Mom, I swear I'll be back by noon, in time to give Kira lunch and get her off to her ballet lesson—I mean, if you have an hour or two you can spare me…"

"Well, I—"

"Thanks." He grabbed her in a hug. "You're a life-saver. I won't be long, I promise." He got his coat from the closet and grabbed his keys from the entry table.

"Matthew…"

"Thanks. I owe you." He closed the door before she could ask him any more questions, thinking how he'd just added lying to his mother to his list of crappy behaviors lately.

Too bad. He'd seen his chance to get Corrie alone and he was damn well taking it.

Since it was Saturday, traffic was light. The drive to her house took fifteen minutes.

He was on her porch with the key to her front door in his hand, ready to let himself in, when he caught himself. It just wasn't right and he knew it. To bust in on her. She'd given him her key in case of emergency, not so he could break in and force her to talk to him. He'd probably scare ten years off her life, sneaking into her house when she wasn't expecting him.

Was she still sleeping? Now, that would be truly creepy of him, appearing in her bedroom, waking her up from a sound asleep. Echoes of dear old dad.

No wonder his mom had fled to Corrie's house, where Davis didn't have a key—and yes, okay. He was willing to go pretty low to get Corrie talking to him again. But not *that* low.

Matt pocketed the key and rang the bell—twice. The second time, he saw the blinds move at the front window and knew she'd spotted him. He was out of luck. Again.

But then, incredibly, he heard the deadbolt turn and there she was in a fuzzy yellow robe and slippers to match. She had last night's makeup smudged around her eyes and serious bed head. She did not look happy, but she did step aside so he could enter.

She shut the door and raked her hair back off her face. "What did you tell your mom?"

"That I needed to pick something up at the office."

"Liar."

He confessed all. "I said it might take a while, that there could be research."

"Research?"

"That was her response, exactly."

She glared at him. "I haven't returned your calls because I didn't want to talk to you."

"I know."

She wrapped her robe tighter, retied the sash. "I guess I can't go on not talking to you forever."

"I'm so damned relieved to hear you say that."

"So. Want some coffee?"

"I do. I really do."

She led him into her warm, comfortable kitchen and gestured in the general direction of the table. He sat down and she loaded up the coffeemaker. Neither of them spoke till the coffee was made.

Then she poured them each a mug full and sat down opposite him, sliding his across to him along with a plate containing two slices of what he recognized as his mother's amazing orange nut bread.

She let him eat half a slice of the bread and sip a little coffee before she said, "There's not much to tell. I went to see Bob. I told him that I'd slept with you and then I gave him back his ring."

"He didn't argue?"

"No, Matt. He didn't."

"What a fool."

She laughed. The sound had more sadness than humor in it. "It wouldn't have mattered what he said. If he was the right guy for me, I wouldn't have done what I did with you."

He agreed with her. But he knew she wouldn't like it much if he said so. "Are you…okay?"

She had the mug in both hands. She shrugged and sipped simultaneously. "I am okay, to tell the ugly truth. I guess that's just more proof that Bob and I were not a very good idea."

"Can we be friends again?"

"I never stopped being your friend."

"Come on, Corrie. You know what I mean."

She tipped her head to the side and looked at him for a long time, wearing a far-away expression he didn't know how to read. "Okay. If you need to hear it, we can be friends again."

"Damn. I'm glad."

"Yeah?"

"Yeah."

She laughed then. A happier laugh than before. "So that's settled." He wanted to reach across the table and take her hand. Or better yet, get up, go to her, pull her out of the chair and wrap his arms around her good and tight. But then, if he did that, he would want to kiss her. And if he kissed her...

Maybe he shouldn't be thinking about that. About kissing her. About what he might do after he kissed her. But he was. Since what had happened between them last Sunday night, he was going to have some trouble *not* thinking about kissing her.

Sunday night had changed everything. Now she was free. There was no reason he couldn't kiss her if he wanted to—unless she turned him down.

And there was only one way to find out about that. He said, "Thank you. For letting my mom stay with you."

"No need for thanks. She's been a godsend, seriously. She cooks most of the meals. And she's been watching Kira for me at night."

"What about Sandra?"

"Sandra quit. She went back to Dallas and stayed

there—which reminds me that one of these days I need to find a replacement."

"If you get stuck, I'll be happy to take Kira."

"I appreciate that." She got up and went to the counter to refill her mug. "More?" She held out the pot.

"Sure."

She came to him and refilled his mug, her robe brushing against him, the scent of her teasing him. She smelled good. She always had. He considered making his move. But on second thought, maybe not while she was holding a pot of scalding coffee. He watched her as she turned, set the pot on the warming ring and then went back to her seat at the table.

He didn't realize she'd guessed what he was thinking until she said, "Forget about it, Matt." Her voice was flat. Her eyes gave him nothing. He wondered whether she meant forget about it for right now—or forever.

He decided not to ask. "Guess I should get back." His chair scraped the floor as he stood.

She sat very still. "You didn't finish your coffee."

"Are you saying you want me to stay?"

She fiddled with her coffee mug, turning it in a circle, sticking her finger through the handle but not raising it to drink. "I want things back like they were before last Sunday."

He almost told her that was fine with him. But then he decided he wasn't willing to lie. "Sorry. No can do."

"I feel like I lost my best friend, you know?"

"You didn't lose me. I'm right here."

She made a soft scoffing noise—and looked away.

He called it as he saw it. "I want you, Corrie. After last Sunday, I'm not going to pretend anymore that I don't."

She met his eyes again. "That's what this has been, the last five years? You, pretending?"

"That's not fair. I've been a good father. A responsible father. And a good friend to you. A *best* friend, you just said so."

She wanted to be mad. He could see that in the stiffness of her shoulders and the set of her jaw. But then she sighed. "Let's not fight. Didn't we just make up?"

He went to her. She tipped her head back to gaze up at him. He held down his hand and said, "I don't want to fight." Her eyes spoke of doubt and even distrust, but she did take his hand. He pulled her up, wrapped his arms around her and gathered her close.

She tipped her head back to look at him and laid her palm, so lightly, fingers spread, against his chest. He felt that gentle touch all the way down to his toes. Now, her eyes were soft. "It's only…look how good we have it. Everything's working out. We're doing an excellent job with Kira. She's happy. I'm happy. You're happy. Why mess with the program?"

He lowered his mouth to kiss her, but she craned back, not allowing their lips to meet. Damn. Evidently, she needed more persuading. Fair enough. "This takes nothing away from what we've got. It only…adds another dimension."

She gave a husky little laugh. "For a bean-counting corporate guy, you're very convincing."

He bent closer, so their lips were only an inch or two

apart. He considered trying again for a kiss, but decided to wait. Next time he made his move, he wanted her ready. And totally willing. "I'll explain again…."

"Oh, I'm sure you will."

"A bean counter is a bookkeeper. Or an accountant. I'm in finance."

"That's right." Her voice was low and lazy. "Finance."

"I don't count the beans. I make decisions about how to spend them. And I find the people who have the beans and help to convince them to invest their beans in Bravo-Corp projects."

"I'll remember that."

"No, you won't. You never do."

"Well, okay." She fiddled with a button on his shirt. "I admit it. I really do enjoy giving you a hard time about your job. And I think it's good for you."

"Good for me, how?"

"Keeps you from getting all fat-headed with self-importance. You don't want to end up like your dad, do you?"

"God, no."

"You need me to keep you humble."

He could think of a lot of things he needed her for. Keeping him humble wasn't one of them. "Corrie…" He pressed his forehead to hers.

"Hmm?"

Words deserted him. But that was okay. She'd tipped her head up and she was looking at him. Her eyes were deep blue velvet and her mouth was softly parted. Welcoming. Ready.

Matt seized the moment. He lowered his head and

captured her lips. That time, instead of pushing him away, her hands slid up to wrap around his neck and a willing sigh escaped her.

Chapter Four

It was a great kiss. A perfect kiss, long and wet and sweet and deep. A kiss that tasted of coffee. And desire. A kiss of promise.

When he lifted his head, she gazed up at him through lazy-lidded eyes. "I forgot to ask."

"Anything…"

"What about Tabby? Are you two on now, or off?"

"Off. Permanently."

"Does Tabby know that?"

He touched the side of her face. Silky-soft. "Tabby and I called it quits three weeks ago. I told you about it, remember? She called me an insensitive, self-centered bastard and said she never wanted to see me again?"

"She's said that before."

"This time it's for real." He lowered his head to steal another kiss.

She stopped him by slipping her hand between them. The pads of her fingers brushed his lips. "I'll think about it."

"About what?"

"You know what. You and me, adding that whole new dimension. Again."

He caught her hand, kissed the tips of her fingers one by one. "You'll think about it…"

"That's right." She stepped back.

With reluctance, he let her go. "Well, okay. It's a start."

Corrine did think about it.

She thought about it way too much, all that day and into the evening. At the Rose, it was extra busy, even for a Saturday. She had to fill in for a bartender who was out sick and messed up more than one drink order because her mind was on Matt instead of on the job where it belonged. Somehow, though, she made it through the night.

At five of three, she was home at last. And there was a late-model black Cadillac parked in her driveway. She could guess who it belonged to.

Davis. Still there at three in the morning. Maybe Aleta wanted him there. Or maybe the pushy SOB had simply showed up, talked his way into the house—and then refused to leave.

Well. Only one way to find out which. A shiver of dread raced along the surface of her skin at the thought of confronting Davis. But hey, if it had to be done, so be it.

There was still room in the driveway for her car to get

by the Caddy. She pulled into the garage and went in through the kitchen. The house was quiet. Aleta had left a light on in the front hall, the way she always did. Such a thoughtful woman. Even if she was married to a total ass. Corrine switched off the hall light and climbed the stairs.

The door to the spare room was shut. She hesitated, her hand raised to knock. Aleta had said she would fight her own battles with Davis. But still, the man had zero conception of the meaning of "no."

Corrine knocked. "Aleta?"

After a moment, she heard stirring in there. A man spoke low.

And then Aleta called, in a sleepy, contented voice, "I'll be right out."

Corrine started to feel a little foolish. "Just, um, checking, to see if everything's okay."

"Everything's okay, truly." Aleta sounded like she meant it.

"All right then, good night." Corrine turned away without waiting for a response.

She tiptoed along the hall and slipped into her room, shutting the door as quietly as she could. With a long, weary sigh, she dropped to the end of the bed, took off her shoes and massaged her aching feet.

The hesitant tap on the door came as she was about to hit the shower. "Yes?" The door opened a crack and Aleta peered around the edge of it. Corrine forced a bright smile. "Come in."

Matt's mother shut the door behind her. She was wearing a silver-gray silk nightgown with a lacy peignoir to match. She looked, well, pretty hot, with her

CHRISTINE RIMMER 63

usually-sleek hair a little mussed and her cheeks slightly flushed. Apparently, she and Davis had been doing the wild thing. Corrine was not in the least hung up about sex. But still, somehow, she'd never thought of Matt's parents having it. Even if they did have nine kids. Seeing Aleta all flushed and satisfied-looking…well, it was just more information than Corrine needed.

Aleta sat on the end of the bed next to her. "I'm so sorry. I meant to have him out of here before you came home. We…" Aleta smoothed her hair. She was actually blushing. "Ahem. We fell asleep."

Corrine swayed to the side enough to nudge Aleta's shoulder. "No need for apologies. If you want him here, he's welcome."

Aleta took her hand, gave it a squeeze. "I know you dislike him." Corrine settled for a shrug over a lying denial. And Aleta said, "I'll wake him up and send him home."

"No."

"Corrine—"

"Shh. I said no. Let him stay. It's okay."

"You're sure?"

"Positive." She forced a bright smile. "So. Is this it? Are you getting back together?"

Aleta took a moment to answer. "I'm still confused, you know? Not sure."

Corrine thought of Matt. "Believe me, I know how that goes."

"I'm not ready to go back to him yet. I need time."

"But you want to see him, to…date him?"

Aleta chuckled. "Date him? How strange to think of dating my own husband. But yes. I want us to be together.

But not all the time. At least not yet." She gave Corrine's hand another squeeze, and then wrapped her arm around her. "Which is why I'm thinking I should move out. Because I know you don't care for him—and for good reason. He's never behaved well when it comes to you, though he's promised me he sees the light on that score."

Corrine grunted. "I'll believe it when I see it."

"And I do understand your skepticism. But the point is, wherever I am, he's going to be around. Until I move back home—or break it off for good."

"Stay."

"It's too much to ask of you."

"No, it's not. I don't like him, but I can put up with him. And if you stay here, you're in a place he has no claim on, a place he can't *get* a claim on. It gives you power. And we girls, we need our power."

"Well said. And I agree completely. But I could find another place where he has no power over me. It's not as if I'm destitute. I do have plenty of money of my own, you know."

Corrine did know. "You were born a Randall. And the Randalls are very big dogs in SA, big dogs with a whole bunch of bucks."

Aleta grinned. "Exactly. I've always had my own money, my own accounts and investments. And I inherited even more when my parents passed on. I could so easily buy myself a place—or simply rent one, for that matter."

"But why go to all that trouble, when you can just stay here until you're sure of what you want to do? Plus, here you have me and Kira. Much nicer than living alone, don't you think?"

Aleta let out a slow sigh. "You're certainly right about that."

"Yes, I am. And don't worry. If Davis drives me too crazy, I can just go to Matt's." Corrine said it and then realized what she was doing. Setting up an excuse to go to him. How pathetic was that? She added, too casually, "Or something."

"Of course you could. Matt has plenty of room..." Aleta's expression was downright angelic. If she knew what was going on between Matt and Corrine lately, she was staying out of it.

"And then there's your nut bread. You don't want to deny me that. Let alone having to find a new nighttime sitter for your granddaughter. You should let me put that off as long as possible."

"You do have a point there."

"Say yes."

"Oh, Corrine..."

"Come on. Say it."

"If you're sure..."

"I'm sure, I'm sure. Bottom line, I love having you here. And Kira loves having you here. Since you've been here, I don't miss my mom quite so much. What else is there to say?"

Aleta's arm tightened around her shoulder. "Sometimes I feel like you're one of my daughters. You know, don't you, that whenever you need me, you only have to tell me so."

Aleta's gentle words warmed her heart and brought

her mom to mind. No doubt, in heaven, Kathleen Lonnigan was smiling to know that her daughter had another "mom" watching out for her. "Good, then. It's settled. You're staying."

When Corrine woke up at eleven the next morning, Davis had already left, which was just fine with her. She would put up with him for Aleta's sake when she had to—and be grateful when she didn't.

Corrine considered going to the afternoon service at New Life Unification Church. But really, she needed to move on, find another church. This time she wouldn't make the mistake of getting romantic with the pastor. So she chose another church at random from the phone book.

It wasn't all that comforting, sitting by herself in a pew among strangers. Plus, the sermon was on the same topic Bob would be preaching on that day: sin and forgiveness. It kind of made her wonder if God was trying to tell her something.

At home, she found a note from Aleta on the kitchen table. Davis was flying her to Vegas overnight. She would be back Monday afternoon, she said. She'd left Corrine's dinner in the fridge. Corrine smiled at that. Aleta, jetting off to Sin City with her rich lover who just happened to be her husband—but remembering to fix dinner for Corrine first.

Matt rang the doorbell at nine. She called, as always, "Come on in!" He paused in the doorway to the living room. They nodded at each other. Then he carried their sleeping daughter up the stairs and tucked her in bed. Just like every Sunday.

Except it wasn't. Since last Sunday, everything had changed.

He came back down. She was sitting on the couch, wearing old sweats and a purple velour hoodie she'd had before Kira was born, her knees drawn up under her chin—just like last Sunday.

Only not.

He came into the living room, tossed his jacket on the chair he'd sat in the Sunday before and went to stand with his back to the fire. She resisted the urge to turn away, to avoid meeting those cloud-gray eyes of his. Instead, she looked at him levelly, a no-nonsense glance that somehow turned hot.

And hungry.

Energy arced between them. That special, intimate kind of electricity that happens between two people who want each other, bad. Never once had she and Bob exchanged such a glance. That probably should have been a serious red flag for her. But no. It had taken a drunken night of great sex in Matt's arms for her to get with the reality that she and Bob were not going to happen.

"Where's Mom?" he asked roughly, his gaze locked tight with hers, caressing her without laying a finger on her.

What was it about him that did it for her, that could weaken her knees and turn a definite no to an eager yes? He was handsome and fit, yeah. But lots of guys were well-built and good-looking. And really, he was kind of stuffy when you came right down to it. Before him, she'd gone for the bad-boy, dangerous types. And after him…?

It hurt her pride to admit it. After all, she had her wild

girl rep to maintain. But there hadn't been anyone after him. Not until sweet, understanding Bob, who didn't believe in sex before marriage.

"Corrie?" His brows had drawn together in a frown.

She knew she'd gone too long without answering. "Sorry. Just thinking."

A knowing smile tipped one corner of that mouth she wanted way too much to kiss. "Thinking about what?"

She ignored that question and answered the one he'd asked before it. "Your mom went to Vegas overnight. With your dad."

He made a low sound of disbelief. "You're joking."

"Nope. I came home from work Saturday, late, and his car was in the driveway."

"So they're reconciling?"

"It's starting to look likely."

"But she's still staying with you?"

"For the time being anyway. She's not completely sure about what she wants to do. They're dating."

He let out a bark of surprised laughter. "My mother and father. Dating."

"That's right."

"Too weird."

"Gotta agree with you there."

He seemed to be studying her. "Maybe that's what we need."

She felt instantly suspicious. "To date, me and you?"

"Yeah. To date. Me and you."

She waved a hand. "You're just trying to get me in bed."

He left the fire then and approached her. Slowly. With caution and also with clear purpose. "Yeah," he said in that low, rough voice that sent her senses spinning. "I am, absolutely, trying to get you into bed." He bent at the waist and put his big, strong hands on the back of the couch, one on either side of her. "I thought I made that pretty damn clear yesterday morning." He smelled so clean and masculine. His irises looked silvery this close up. Silver ringed with blue and rayed with golden-brown.

For almost five years, she'd had herself convinced she was over him, that they were friends. Good friends. *Best* friends. And then last Sunday came along and blew that lie wide open.

She was kind of mad at him about that, really. Hadn't he done enough six years ago, setting her whole world on its ear the way he had? Did he have to do it all over again?

"Matt…" His name came out of her mouth on a yearning sigh. She forgot whatever she'd meant to say. Probably *no* or maybe *stop*.

But then he bent closer and he was kissing her and words like no and stop didn't even exist anymore. He sank down to the couch beside her and gathered her into his big, strong arms.

She kissed him back. With eagerness and longing. She let her hands roam over his muscled shoulders and up into the close-cropped hair at his nape. It felt so good. *Too* good to be all wrapped up in his arms. Again. It seemed like forever since she'd felt his lips on hers.

But then he eased his hand up under the purple hoodie and captured her breast. A bolt of hot lightning speared through her. She moaned into his mouth.

And then she remembered to act like she had a brain.

She grabbed his hard shoulders and pushed him back, demanding flatly, "Got condoms?"

"In my pocket."

Damn. "So much for that excuse."

He touched the side of her face, a tender caress that made her almost feel sorry for pushing him away. "You're killing me, you know that?"

She steeled her resolve, not sure why she didn't just surrender to the inevitable. Except that, along with the burning desire she felt for him, there was resentment. And disappointment at herself, to be giving her body and her senses into his hands all over again. You'd think she would have learned her lesson the first time. "Buck up. You'll live."

An answering spark of anger flashed in his eyes. And then he let her go and slid away to the other end of the couch. "All right. I'm over here. You're over there. Is that what you wanted?"

It wasn't, not really. "Sorry. I'm feeling a little…conflicted, I guess."

"Maybe more than a little." His voice had gentled, too.

"Yeah. All right. Maybe so."

He leaned forward, braced his elbows on his spread knees and tipped his head to the side to look at her. His shirt clung lovingly to the strong muscles of his back. She longed to reach out, touch him, pull him close again.

Conflicted. For sure.

He asked, "What time does Mom get back tomorrow?"

"The note she left said in the afternoon."

"Great. Tomorrow the Rose is closed. You don't have to work. And Mom can watch Kira."

"Why?"

"Suddenly you've become the most suspicious damn woman in Texas."

"Why?"

"We're going out to dinner, you and me."

Okay, that sounded kind of wonderful. Just the two of them, in a nice restaurant, a place with white table-cloths and real napkins. And maybe a bud vase with a single rose. And candles. Dinner was so romantic by candlelight.

She remembered she was still conflicted. "Now you're giving me instructions."

"Yeah, I am. We're going someplace really expensive. Because I'm rich and money is no object."

She sighed. "Well, okay. You *are* tempting me."

"That was the idea. I'll pick you up at seven. Wear something low-cut and sexy. At least let me look if I'm not allowed to touch."

Chapter Five

Matt had a plan. He thought it was a really excellent plan. True, it scared the crap out of him.

But he thought it was the *right* plan. The plan he knew Corrie wanted, deep in her heart. The plan that was best for everyone concerned.

When he got to her house Monday evening, his mom answered the door. "Matthew. Hello. Don't you look handsome?" She leaned forward and presented her cheek. He kissed it and she ushered him inside.

He asked, "So how was Vegas?"

"Wonderful." Her smile gave nothing away.

"How much did you lose?"

She clucked her tongue at him. "I *always* win." He thought she looked…different. More confident somehow.

More sure of herself than in the past. Not that she'd lacked confidence before, exactly.

As he tried to understand the strange changes in his mother, his daughter came flying down the stairs with her arms out. "Daddy!" She launched herself at him and he caught her, lifting her up so she could wrap her legs around his waist. "Hi!" She kissed him, loudly, on the cheek.

"How's my girl?"

The question was all the encouragement Kira needed. "The teacher put my picture of the pilgrims and the Native 'Mericans on the bulletin board."

"Excellent."

"There was corn and turkey in the picture. It was the first Thanksgiving, what I drew. The pilgrims' hats were *hard* to draw. But they turned out pretty good. Then we did alphabet games and we did adding. And we had recess, too. We always have recess. And cookies and milk. And naps."

"Sounds like a perfect day at school."

"And then I had my tap-dancing lesson. And then Gramma picked me up and we...Daddy." She put her two soft hands on either side of his face and steered it in her direction. "Listen to me, Daddy."

"I am, sweetheart." But he wasn't. Corrie was coming down the stairs. She wore a blue dress that clung to every curve. And her shining blond hair dipped over one eye, just the way he liked it best.

"Daddy..."

He gave Kira a kiss on the cheek. "I'm glad you had a great day."

"I did. It was a very nice day."

"Good. And I'm so proud of you." He eased her down to the floor again. By then, Corrie was right behind her.

Kira turned. "Mommy." She clapped her hands. "You look so pretty."

"Thank you, baby."

His mom said, "Kira, honey. Kiss your mommy goodbye. She and Daddy are going out to dinner."

Kira beamed. "I could go, too. We could go to Chuck E. Cheese's."

"You already ate, remember? Besides, it's an adult night," his mom explained.

"'Dolts? I like 'dolts."

All the 'dolts were careful not to laugh and his mom corrected her gently. "A-dults. That means grown-ups. And tonight, your mommy and daddy will be out past your bedtime."

Kira sagged in five-year-old disappointment. "Oh, pleeeeease. I *really* want to go…."

Matt offered, "Another time, sweetheart."

His daughter was nothing if not ready to bargain. "All of us? You and me and Mom and Gramma, too?"

"That's right. Maybe next Sunday."

"Sunday?" Kira moaned. "It's days and days until Sunday."

"Don't push it," he said and tried to sound stern.

Kira was a smart kid. She knew when to give it up. "Oh, all right. Next Sunday. We can have a deal." She offered her hand. Matt took it and gave it a shake. Then she reached up her arms to Corrie and kissed her cheek as loudly as she'd kissed his.

"'Night," said his mom. "Come on, honey." She steered Kira into the living room.

Corrie got her coat from the closet by the door and he helped her into it, bending closer than he needed to, letting the scent of her hair tempt him and the warmth of her skin make him long to turn her around and wrap his arms around her.

He restrained himself, remembering the night before when she'd pushed him away for moving too fast. Later. After a decent steak and a little wine. After he executed his excellent plan.

She grabbed a small, sparkly purse off the chair by the door and they were out of there.

He took her to the best steak house in town, a two-story place in a converted silo. The bar was on the ground floor and the restaurant upstairs. The maitre d' took Corrie's coat and then led them up the curving stairs to their table, which was covered with snowy linen and set with fat white candles in crystal bowls. Corrie looked beautiful by candlelight, her blue eyes shining like sapphires, her skin creamy pink.

He ordered a nice bottle of wine and they chose an appetizer and, for the main course, filet mignon.

Once the waiter had poured the wine and left them alone, Corrie let out a contented sigh. "Matt. I hardly believe this. Seven-thirty on a weeknight and you're not working."

He gave a wry nod. "Yeah, okay. I admit it. I've been pretty much a workaholic."

Her expression got softer. He thought about rising

enough to lean across the table and claim her mouth in a kiss—but no, he reminded himself. Not yet.

Not yet...

She said, "I wasn't complaining. You always saved the weekends for Kira. And that's what matters—though I have wondered how you made time for Tabby...."

"Can we forget Tabby? Please?"

She laughed, a low, husky sound. "When you say please like that, you remind me of Kira, begging to go to Chuck E. Cheese's."

He grunted. "Is that good?"

"It is. It's charming. And very sweet."

"I'm flattered. I guess—and I mean it. Can we forget Tabby?"

She nodded. "You're right. We're having a nice evening out together and Tabby Ellison has no business here. She's forgotten—but I *would* like to know..."

"Anything." He was feeling expansive, with his plan in place and Corrie sitting across from him, out on their first real date in almost six years.

She asked, "What made you decide to stop and smell the roses?"

"You got engaged to Pastor Bob."

She blinked. "You're kidding."

He wasn't. Not in the least. But the way she was looking at him—both surprised and disbelieving—made him uncomfortable. So he backpedaled a little. "Well, I mean, until you got together with Bob, I was kind of used to the way things were going. But then, when you decided to marry him, I started seeing that everything would change, that nothing in this life is a given, there are no guarantees. And…I don't know. What is it they say? That when a man's on his deathbed, chances are the last thing he'll regret is that he didn't spend more time at work."

She sat back in her chair and folded her hands in her lap. "Well. Good for you, Matt."

He felt a little foolish. Had he sounded like a wimp or something? "Yeah, well. I'm not the deepest guy around, but I'm working on it."

Now she sat forward. Her eyes shone with what might have been approval. "You're the greatest."

Pleasure filled him. "Uh. I am?"

"You are. I have to admit…" Whatever she'd been about to say, she was reconsidering it. She glanced away and then back again.

"What? Tell me."

"When I found out I was pregnant with Kira?"

He leaned in close, too. "Yeah?"

"I was so scared. I knew I would keep the baby. I was raised Catholic, even if I've completely lapsed. But I didn't know how you would take it. I never expected for things to turn out the way they have."

"And how's that?"

"You're a wonderful dad, Matt. You really are. And the best friend a single mom could have."

"You mean that?"

"Mmm-hmm."

Damn, it felt good. To hear her say it. Again, he considered executing the plan, right then and there. But no. Later. At his place. When they were alone.

He thanked her. The waiter came with their appetizers. They talked and laughed about everyday things. Kira's artistic abilities—they both agreed their daughter could draw a mean stick figure. And the upcoming Thanksgiving play at Kira's school. She would be a pilgrim and she'd already made her pilgrim hat from black construction paper.

"Your dad wants to go," she told him.

"To the school play?"

She nodded. "He and your mom talked about it during their weekend in Vegas. She asked me if maybe we could all go together."

"Could you stand being in the same car with him?"

She smiled. "Your mom asked the same question."

"Well?"

"They're seeing each other. He's going to be around a lot. And anyway, he's always civil to me. At least in the past few years."

Matt laughed. "You should see your face. Like you just sucked a lemon. He's still not your favorite person."

"No, and I doubt he'll ever be—but yes, I can bear a car ride with him as long as he behaves himself."

Matt took her meaning. Davis had said some really low things about Corrie in the past. Once, a few months after Kira was born, Matt had gotten so mad over it, he'd actually punched his dad square in the jaw. Davis hadn't hit him back—and he'd watched his mouth about Corrie from then on. Matt had never told Corrie about busting his dad's chops. She would only have asked what Davis had said to make Matt do such a thing. No way she needed to know that.

The waiter took the appetizer plates away and served the filets. For a few minutes, they ate in silence.

Then he brought up his mom. "She's…different, you know? When she answered the door tonight, she seemed more confident than she used to be. But then, it's not like I've ever thought of her as shy. She's always been strong and capable, and self-assured, too. My God, the woman was not only born with a platinum card in her mouth, she had nine kids, one right after the other, and never let it get her down."

"You think maybe she wonders if your dad married her for her connections and her fortune?"

"How could she? He's wild for her. He always has been. Sometimes, we joke about it, me and my brothers and sisters. That they act like a couple of horny teenagers. More than once I've wanted to tell them to cut it out and get a room."

"I'm just saying, it's not so surprising now, to me, that she left him."

"Uh. It's not?"

"Think about it. She gave him everything. Her heart, her body—nine kids for his damn dynasty, for cryin' out loud—her money and her good name. I'm sure a lot of doors opened for him after he married a Randall."

"Corrie, you're preaching to the choir here. No argument, my dad's a man who wanted it all and made sure he got it. But he did love my mom—he did and he does and he always will."

"Still, he screwed around on her with Javier Cabrera's wife."

"He needs a lot of…attention, my dad. And my mom

was busy with all of us. When the thing happened with Luz, she hardly had time for him."

Corrie wasn't the least impressed with his dad's need for attention. "Busy?" she scoffed. "Your mom was *busy?* She had to be flat-out exhausted, doing her best to do right by her children. She needed her husband to be there for her then. *She* was the one who deserved a little love and attention. But what does she get? Her husband goes out and puts it to someone else's wife."

"My mother said all that?"

"More or less. In her own words. But even if she hadn't, it's self-evident. Think about it. Who wanted all those kids?"

"Corrie, they both did."

"He wanted a dynasty. You've told me that yourself. He wanted to have seven sons like *his* father did—only *he* wasn't going to chase them all away."

He put up both hands. "I surrender."

"He cheated, pure and simple!" She practically shouted the word. And then she winced and shot a glance around the restaurant. One or two people had looked their way but then quickly turned back to their own dinner companions. Her cheeks flushing with embarrassment, she spoke in a near-whisper, leaning in toward him. "Oops. I think I kind of got carried away."

He chuckled. "Are you *sure* you're going to manage riding to Kira's Thanksgiving play in the same car as my dad?"

She picked up her fork and knife. "Like I said, as long as he behaves himself, I've got no problem with him."

"Well, except that you hate him."

"I never said that. And I *don't* hate him. I just…" She let the sentence trail away with a shake of her golden head.

Matt spoke gently. "He's treated you like crap, I know it. But that was in the past, right? He hasn't given you any trouble lately, has he?" He'd better not have or Matt would be giving *him* trouble. And plenty of it.

She set down her knife and waved a hand. "No. And I'm sorry. I get a little over the top when I start talking about him, I guess." She sipped from her water glass and then sat back with a sigh. "I'm stuffed."

"You know this place is famous for their lava cake?"

She groaned. "It's really mean of you to tempt me like that."

He wanted to tempt her, all right. And with a lot more than the lava cake. "We could order one and ask for two spoons…."

The waiter brought them the dark-chocolate cake with vanilla-bean ice cream on top and hot fudge sauce oozing out from below. Matt watched her take a spoonful, enjoying the look of bliss on her face as the rich flavors filled her mouth.

She saw him watching. "Get to work. It's bad enough I couldn't resist letting you order this. No way I'm eating it all by myself."

Matt ate the cake—more than half of it, actually. It was really good. But even better was sitting there across from Corrie, watching the way the candlelight shone on her hair, listening to her sigh as she took each sinful bite.

When the shared plate was empty, she set down her spoon with a little groan of satisfaction. "That was fabulous. All of it—and I realize I got so wrapped up in ragging on your father, I never got to agree with what you said about your mom seeming more confident."

"You noticed, too?"

"Yeah. And I think she *is* more confident. In your father's love. Deep inside, she's always wondered if he loved her anywhere near as much as she loved him. Slowly, I think he's convincing her that he does, that she means the world to him."

"That's good."

"Yeah. I think it is, too. Your mom loves him. And even though I don't care for him much myself, I want her to be happy."

"So then, is she moving back to Olmos Park?"

"She told me no, not yet."

"What the hell. You just said—"

"Matt. She's having a great time. And she's not ready to go back to him yet, to settle into being a couple of old married folks again. Let it...unfold, you know?"

"Unfold?"

"Whatever. You know what I mean."

"But you think she will go back to him eventually?"

"My opinion? Absolutely. But I guess we'll never know for sure until it happens."

After the meal they stopped on the chilly, darkened street outside.

"Will you look at that?" Matt pointed at the street-light nearby. It had a wreath attached beneath the lamp, a wreath with three red electric candles in the center. "They've got the Christmas decorations up already. And it's not even Thanksgiving."

She took his arm. "I like them. They're pretty and bright. Please don't start in about how it's so crass and commercial."

He stared into her upturned face. "Well, all right. If you think they're pretty, they're just fine with me."

"Merry Christmas and a big ho-ho-ho." She kissed his cheek, a smacking kiss, the kind their daughter always gave him.

"Hey," he teased, pulling her fully into his embrace. "You can do better than that."

Her eyes were blue diamonds. "Think so, huh?"

"I know so." He lowered his head. Wonder of wonders, she lifted her lips to meet his. They shared a long, deep kiss, right there on the sidewalk. When they came up for air, he whispered, "Come to my place with me."

He was absolutely certain she would tell him no. But she didn't.

She held his gaze and softly answered, "Yes."

Chapter Six

Corrie had already admitted to herself that she and Matt were heading toward a second love affair.

Still, maybe she should have held him off a little longer. Maybe if she'd put him off for a while, they would both decide it was just too risky and come to their senses. Go back to life as they had known it, which was pretty damn good and could easily be messed up beyond repair by this complete foolishness they both seemed determined to surrender to.

Tonight.

Oh, God.

Tonight.

She was a bundle of nerves as he drove to his place. The tension only ratcheted higher when he unlocked the front door and ushered her in ahead of him. He punched the code into the alarm but left the lights in the high-ceilinged foyer as they were: dim but enough to see by.

He turned to her and took her in his arms. They shared another of those endless kisses that made her knees wobbly and her mind a blur of erotic images. She clung to him, hopelessly aroused, as he eased her coat off her shoulders and dropped it on a chair. She gave him her purse and he put it with the coat.

Then he took her hand. "Come on."

Their footsteps echoed on the slate floor as he led her to the wide staircase and up.

In his room, which had a platform bed the size of Kansas and acres of bamboo flooring, the lights were set at the same low, shadowed level as downstairs. He touched a panel by the door and they glowed a little brighter.

He caught her face between his hands. "You have no idea how long I've waited for tonight."

She teased him, "After all, it's been a whole week…."

He framed her face with his hands. "That's not what I meant."

"Oh, no?"

"Uh-uh." His gray eyes held her captive. "Last week you were engaged."

And now I'm not. Whose fault is that? The words were there, in her mind. But why say them? Why even *think* them? In the end, she knew the blame belonged to her. He'd only helped her to face the hard truth that she and Bob were not a match.

"Well," she told him softly. "I'm not engaged now."

"Exactly my point…" The words trailed off. She saw in his eyes that he was about to say more. But he didn't.

He only cradled her face in his hands and gazed at her as if he needed to commit her features to memory.

"What is it?" she asked at last.

He shook his head. "Nothing. Kiss me."

She lifted her mouth. He took it and she drowned in lovely, arousing sensation once more. When he raised his head that time, he lowered his hands to her shoulders. Slowly, he walked her backward until her legs touched the thick mattress on the bed.

The blankets were already turned neatly down, no doubt by his housekeeper, a middle-aged German woman who worked hard and rarely spoke. Corrine felt the smooth sheet at the back of her knees and she wanted to be naked on that sheet, with him. Sliding her hands down the sides of her hips, she began to gather up the silky fabric of her blue dress.

She stopped at mid-thigh, asked, "More?"

"Please." He stepped back to get a better view.

Inch by slow inch, she eased her skirt higher, revealing her bare legs all the way up to her blue thong. And higher. Once she had the dress to waist height, she caught the hem and whipped it up and over her head, tossing it away. It landed on the floor somewhere past the end of the bed. Then she straightened her shoulders and stood proudly before him in her shoes, her underwear, her heart-shaped diamond navel ring and nothing more.

He whispered, "Now that's what I'm talkin' about…"

She reached behind her, unhooked her blue bra and anchored it against her breasts with her free arm as she eased the straps down one bare shoulder and then the other. With a teasing glance at him from under her lashes, she whipped the bra away and sent it sailing in the same direction as her dress. She took her time stepping out of the thong. He watched every move she made, gray gaze never wavering. She had his complete attention as she kicked her blue satin high heels away and heard them slide and skitter across the floor.

He put out a hand and tugged lightly on the diamond heart suspended from her navel. "You are so damn beautiful." He said the words low in his throat, a rough sound that told her how much he wanted her.

"You always said that." Her own throat felt clogged, suddenly, with feelings she didn't dare give a name.

"And I meant it. You are. The most beautiful woman I've ever known." His gaze moved over her, lingering on the faint white stretch marks at either side of her hips, testimony to the fact that she'd carried their child. "From Kira?"

She nodded, swallowing, trying to banish the hard knot of emotion that threatened to overwhelm her as he touched her again, tracing those pale lines with the pad of a finger. His touch was warm, knowing. Too well-remembered.

His gaze held hers, intimate. Tender. And all at once, she was recalling the day she had Kira. The sweat and the pain and the blood and the screaming—her own screaming. Matt had been with her that day. He'd insisted he would be there, though she'd told him she didn't need him and he didn't have to bother.

But her mom had called him against her orders when she went into active labor. She remembered the moment he appeared, sticking his head in the door of the labor room. She'd shot her mother a scowl. Kathleen

Lonnigan had only smiled sweetly and gone to take Matt's hand, to pull him fully into the room. Into the experience of his daughter being born.

He and her mom took turns sitting by her bed as she labored to bring Kira into the world. She remembered the feel of his big, strong hand holding her sweaty one, remembered the panic in his eyes. He didn't know squat about having babies. And her screaming must have scared him.

But he had stuck with her, spelling her mother at her side. And later, the first time he held their baby, when she saw the look of pure love in his cloud-colored eyes...

It had undone her. She had forgiven him everything at that moment. And just the memory of it was threatening to undo her now.

"Corrie?"

"Hmm?"

"You okay?"

She nodded, swallowed. Hard. "Undress."

He balked. She wasn't surprised. He didn't like being ordered around any more than she did. "First, I want you to—"

"Undress."

"—turn around. Please."

"Why?" She had a pretty good idea of why, actually. But something contrary in her nature had her insisting he say it out loud.

And he did. "Because I want to see that amazing tattoo. I didn't get a good look at it last week. Everything was kind of hazy that night. It happened as if in a dream. A really *good* dream, but a dream nonetheless."

She considered whether to hold the line on him about this, to insist that he take off his clothes first. But then again, what would that gain her except a false feeling of control? It was called making love for a reason, after all. It took two and both of them should be getting what they wanted out of the experience.

If it gave him pleasure to look at her backside…

"Fair enough." She turned and showed him what he wanted to see.

Silence. She stared at a couple of framed prints on the far wall and felt her own nakedness acutely.

Then he said it again. "So damn beautiful." The air in the room shifted as he stepped closer. She felt his touch, starting low on one side, tracing the vines in their curling, dangerous, thorny pattern, pausing to caress the roses, and then moving on. "Tell me again. How you got it…"

"In Mexico, spring break my senior year. Me and three girlfriends. We all decided to get tattoos. Just lucky, I guess, that the guy we went to was a true artist."

"How long did it take?"

"Hours and hours. And it hurt like a sonofagun. My girlfriends all got itty-bitty ladybugs and butterflies. Not me. I was feeling empowered, I guess you could say. I had to make a statement, all the way from my butt halfway up my back."

He made a low, admiring sound and continued tracing the thorny vines, touching the red blooms, until he was brushing the other side of her waist. His hand settled there, clasping.

Claiming. He pulled her in close to him, her back to his front. She felt his body warmth acutely, even through his clothes. His arousal pressed into the tattoo he'd just traced and his breath stirred her hair. The scent of him came to her, pleasing to her, as always. She reached back to wrap her hand around his neck, to feel the warmth of his skin against her palm. And then she turned her head to him.

His mouth settled on hers in a kiss so sweet and deep it made her melt inside.

He turned her around so she faced him again and he touched her breasts, brushing the nipples, one and then the other. And then clasping the left one in a way that was somehow cherishing and so sexy, both at once.

"The night we met…" His thumb flicked, teasing her nipple. "When you turned over and stretched out on your stomach, after that first time we made love…"

"Yeah?"

"Your skin was so smooth, shiny with sweat, and I saw those black vines, the thorns, the deep, red roses…"

"Hmm?" The sound rose from her like a purr from a happy cat.

"I almost came again. Right then and there, out of nowhere."

She couldn't help smiling, remembering. "That was a good night."

"That was a night I'll never forget."

"Well, and how could you? We made Kira that night—which reminds me. Condoms?"

"In the drawer." He gestured toward the nightstand by the head of the bed.

That eased her mind. They didn't need another slipup. "So, then…?"

He knew what she wanted. And he put up no resistance that time. He took a step back and he started peeling off his clothes, tossing them toward a chair several feet away. Some of them hit the mark, some didn't. He didn't seem to care much either way.

When he was naked, she sighed. He'd made a lot of trouble for her in her life, but he'd brought more joy than heartache. After all, he'd given her Kira. And even though he hadn't wanted to marry her back then, well, it wasn't as if she'd expected marriage. Far from it. Once she'd accepted that she would be a single mom, she'd been sure he would fade from her life and her baby's life, too, that she would have to decide whether to track him down for child support or let it go.

How wrong she'd been. She had totally underestimated him. He had stuck by her. No, they weren't married. But he was a hands-on, dedicated dad.

They were a team, really, in their commitment to their little girl. And in their friendship, which had slowly taken form and grown over the years, totally beyond her expectations.

He chuckled low. "You've got that look."

"What look?"

"That sentimental look."

"Naw," she lied. And changed the subject. "I was just thinking that I can understand why you need a gym in your house, after all." He had one in the basement. She'd made fun of it the first time she saw it.

He looked puzzled. "My home gym? You were getting sentimental over my exercise equipment?"

She blew out an impatient breath. "Don't you know a compliment when you hear it?"

"Uh. Guess not."

"Duh. I was thinking how hot you are."

He didn't buy it for a minute. "No, you weren't. You were thinking what a pain in the ass I am, but you're crazy about me anyway."

A burst of laughter escaped her. "You do surprise me sometimes."

He reached out and reeled her in. It was a delicious shock, to feel her naked body pressed to his, her softness against his hardness. "Let me surprise you some more."

She gasped when he slid his hand down between them, skimming her belly, delving into the close-trimmed curls between her thighs, parting her, rubbing her, finding just the right place...

How was it a bean counter knew just the right place? She let her head fall back. She moaned at the ceiling.

"Wet," he whispered, nipping her ear, then licking the side of her neck in one long, slow, thrilling stroke. Below, his fingers worked their special magic. "You're so wet for me. So silky. So sweet..."

She couldn't talk by then. She could only moan and clutch his powerful shoulders and move her hips in rhythm with his caressing hand.

He caught her earlobe between his teeth and bit down just hard enough to multiply the pleasure he was giving her with those knowing, clever fingers of his. "I love the way you smell. The way you move when I'm touching you like this. I love the feel of your skin under my hands...."

It happened so fast—the rising, the soft, pulsing explosion. She fell back to the bed with a cry of fulfillment.

He followed her down, his fingers still touching her, stroking her, increasing the pleasure until it was unbearable it was so good. She tossed her head from side to side, making guttural sounds deep in her throat.

Finally, her climax hit the peak and hovered there. She moaned in satisfaction as the pleasure faded slowly down into a glow of fulfillment.

When she opened her eyes, Matt was stretched out on his side next to her, his head braced on his hand, grinning down at her.

He said, "You're amazing."

And she couldn't help returning his grin. "Me? All I did was moan and wiggle around."

He nuzzled her cheek. "But it's the *way* you moan. And you're so sexy when you wiggle." He traced a caress down the inside of her arm. "We should have done this years ago."

His words brought all her doubts back in full force. They were messing with a damn good relationship, taking a chance they should have known better than to take. "Frankly, we shouldn't be doing this at all."

He put his finger against her mouth. "Shh." She smelled herself on his hand, the musky scent of her arousal. "You're here. I'm here. We're doing this."

She knew he was right. They *were* doing this. Yammering on about how they shouldn't didn't change a thing.

He traced the shape of her nose, and then her eyebrows, and then smoothed her hair back off her forehead. And then he lowered his mouth to hers.

They kissed forever, his tongue delving in, playing with hers, tempting her to follow when he retreated. She did follow. She tasted all the slick surfaces beyond his lips and wondered how she'd gone all those years without lying beside him naked in his arms.

She reached down and encircled him. He groaned into her mouth. And then she was kissing her way along his throat, dipping her tongue into the groove where his collarbones met, going lower, over his strong chest, down his sculpted belly.

And lower still.

She took him in her mouth, loving the slickness, the salty flavor of him, opening wide to take him all the way in and then slowly letting him out again. He rolled to his back, his hands in her hair, holding her close to him as she encircled him tightly with her hand, took him all the way inside her mouth, deep enough to press against the soft arch way in the back of her throat. She loved the way he lifted up to her, the pleasured groans rising from deep in his chest. She teased him, licking the crown as she stroked him with her hand, running her tongue around and around, nipping lightly with her teeth before taking him deep inside again.

He lasted for several minutes as she played with him, as she urged him with lips and tongue and stroking hand to take it all the way to release.

But he wasn't going for that. At what seemed to her the last possible second, he captured her face and made her look at him. "The drawer," he said on a growl. "Get it. Now."

She knew what he meant and scooted over enough to pull the drawer open and dip a hand in. She grabbed one and shoved the drawer shut.

"Give it here," he commanded.

She handed it over and then she couldn't resist the temptation of him, so hard and slick and ready, right there at eye level. As he struggled to get the wrapper off, she encircled him again and sucked him deep into her throat.

He made a strangled sound and pushed at her shoulder. "I want...I need...you..."

She couldn't resist such a desperate plea. By then he had the wrapper off. She moved back enough that he could slide it on.

And then she curved her legs under her and rose up, straddling him. He lay beneath her, so strong and beautiful—beautiful as only a gorgeous man can be. His eyes were shut, his face flushed, his lips pressed together in an expression of need and urgency.

"Corrie..." He opened his eyes and saw her watching him. "Corrie..." He took her waist between his hands.

She rose up enough to position herself. And then, her eyes locked with his, she lowered her body down on his, the descent slow and constant, until she had him within her, fully.

He groaned and lifted his hips for her.

She rode him, moving on him as he rocked beneath her, like a wild horse, a surging wave. Nothing better in her whole life than to be with him this way. He felt so good inside her. So absolutely right.

But then, he always had. They fit, the two of them. They were a perfect match—at least as far as their bodies were concerned. When she was making love with him, she lost herself completely, she drowned in sensation.

His hands slid down to cup her bottom. He rocked her with ever-increasing insistence. She took his cues, gave them back, slow and sweet, then fast and frantic.

When she came, she pressed down hard on him. With a deep groan, he held her tight. She went over. He followed right after, moaning her name.

Sometime later, he left her, disappearing briefly into the bathroom. She heard the toilet flush and water running and thought how she probably ought to get up, find her clothes and ask him to drive her home.

But in the end, she hardly stirred. She stared up at his vaulted ceiling, smiling dreamily, feeling satisfied in the deepest, most delightful way. With a sigh, she rolled over and folded her arms on the pillow, resting her cheek on them.

She felt the bed shift. And then Matt bent close to her. He pressed his lips to the small of her back. "Corrie." His warm breath felt good against her skin.

"Umm?"

He brushed little kisses up the bumps of her spine. Then he blew in her ear. "I have an idea."

She stirred then, reluctantly, turning to him, rising up on an elbow. "An idea, huh?"

"I think it's a great idea. One that makes total sense and is good for everyone." He levered back off his knees to sit with his legs crossed. He looked magnificent naked.

And he was holding one hand behind his back.

She frowned. "Matt. What's that you're hiding?"

"What?" He whipped out a little velvet jewelry box. A ring-sized one. "You mean this?"

This wasn't happening. "Matt. No."

He grinned and flipped the box open. A huge diamond flanked by two slightly smaller ones sparkled at her. "Marry me, Corrie."

Chapter Seven

The first thing Corrine felt at the sight of that giant rock was anger, hot and bright. Irrational anger that made her want to grab that ring box out of his hand and throw it, hard, across the room.

But of course, she didn't. She made herself be still.

He waited, holding out that rock that must have cost a fortune, his expression so hopeful and proud, making her think of Kira for some crazy reason. Kira, on the day she finally learned to tie her shoes.

Look, Mommy! I did it. I did it all by myself!

He had that same look. Of triumph and joy. That he'd finally done the grown man's equivalent of tying his own shoes. He'd decided to marry the mother of his child, after all. Decided all on his own. Even gone out and bought her a ring to die for.

Her anger turned to sadness that she'd been angry at

him in the first place. What was there to be angry about? He was only trying to do the right thing. Finally. After all these years.

She pulled herself to a sitting position, facing him, crossing her legs in a mirror of his pose, and raking her hair back off her face. "Oh, Matt…"

His look of pleasure deepened. He was totally misreading her reaction. "Come on." He pulled the ring free of its satin bed. "Put it on."

"Matt…"

He was all wrapped up in his own excitement, pleased as a kid with his first bicycle. "Give me your hand." He reached out and grabbed her wrist.

She whipped it away from him. "Matt!" She hadn't realized she'd shouted his name until he winced.

He frowned at her, bewildered. "What?" he asked, in a near-whisper. Then, louder, "What?"

"Matt, no."

He blinked. "Uh. No?"

She nodded, swallowed, shook her head. "No."

"But I don't—"

"Look. It's so sweet of you, to want to do this. I'm, well, I'm touched that you would. Deeply touched."

He stared at her as though she was speaking in tongues or something. "So, then, okay. What's the problem? Let's get married." He tried to reach for her hand again.

She backed away. "Matt. I said no. I meant no."

He gaped. "No."

"That's right. No."

For an endless three or four seconds he stared at her.

Then, at last, he stuck the ring back in the box, snapped it shut and set it on the rumpled sheet between them. "All right. I'll bite. Why not?"

I couldn't stand the heartbreak if it didn't work. "Just think, okay? Stop and think about it."

"It? What?"

"We've got it good. Excellent, even. Our daughter is happy. She's never had married parents and it's working out great for her. She doesn't *need* married parents."

"She will," he said darkly. "When she's older, when she begins to understand what she's missing. A family. A mom and dad, together, committed to each other as well as to her."

"But we're already committed to each other. We're best friends. We get along great, we work together to give Kira the best life possible. It can't get any better than it already is."

"Oh, yeah. It can."

"Matt. Come on." She reached out a hand.

He jerked back from her touch. "Come on, what?"

She let her hand drop. With effort, she kept her voice gentle. "Why fix something that isn't broken?"

"That's pretty much what you said about us having sex together again."

"No, I didn't."

"You did. You said why mess with the program. You sorry about making love with me tonight, too?"

"No. Of course not. Tonight has been beautiful. Exciting. Just perfect."

He glanced away, toward the doorway to the sitting area. He seemed to be studying one of the club chairs in there. When he faced her again, he gave a half-shrug, a lazy lift of one muscular shoulder. "It's kind of funny, if you think about it…"

Whatever *it* was, it wasn't the least bit funny. She could tell by his bleak expression. But she asked, anyway, "What's funny?"

"Who knew that *you* would end up being the one unwilling to take a chance?"

Her anger rose again. She tamped it down. "That's not fair."

He shrugged a second time. "Fair or not, it's the truth."

She bit her tongue. What good would it do to argue the point? "It's…lovely of you, really, to offer to marry me, but I—"

He swore. "It's not lovely in the least. It's the best thing, for everyone concerned."

"In your opinion."

"This has nothing to do with my damn opinion. It's the best thing, period. For you, for me and for Kira most of all. Because we *are* a family, no matter how much effort you expend denying it."

"I didn't say we weren't a family in our own way."

"So then do the right thing. Make us a family in every way."

She kept her voice soft and even. "I disagree that marriage, for us, is necessarily the right thing. Can we leave it at that?"

He grunted. "As if I've got a damn choice in the matter."

Matt fumed in silence as he drove Corrie home. When they arrived, his inner gentleman surfaced enough that he offered to walk her up to the door.

"Thanks. There's no need." She got out. He waited in the driveway, the engine idling, to watch over her until she let herself in.

She surprised him by going around the front of the car to his side window. She rapped the glass with her knuckles. He was just ticked off enough at her that he only glared at her, mouth set and eyes narrowed. But then she mouthed the word "Please," and he relented. He pushed the button and the window slid down.

"I had a wonderful evening," she said softly. "I hope we can do this again sometime."

"Damn you, Corrie."

And then she leaned in the window and kissed him. Her lips were cool at first. But they got hot fast.

So did he. He surrendered and kissed her back. Okay, she wouldn't marry him. But at least she was open now about wanting him. Things could be worse.

When she ended the kiss, he got a tender smile and a whispered, "'Night."

Grudgingly, he answered, "'Night."

He was mad all over again by the time he got back to his place. He went upstairs and undressed for the second time that night.

The ring in its velvet box was still there on the white sheet in the middle of the bed. He stuck it in a dresser drawer where he wouldn't have to look at it and got back into bed. The scent of her was on his pillow. He pressed his face against it and breathed in deep, wondering what the hell she'd done to him.

For the rest of the week, he refused to call her. She

didn't call him, either, which completely annoyed him. Saturday, when she brought Kira over, he played it cool.

Unfortunately, so did she. In no time, she had kissed Kira and ducked back out the door, leaving him almost no opportunity to show her how displeased he was with her.

Saturday evening, after Kira was in bed, he thought about calling her at the Rose. Which was totally stupid. She would be busy. It was Saturday night, for God's sake. If he was going to break down and call her, Saturday night was the absolute worst time to do it.

Then the doorbell rang. His heart leapt. He was absolutely certain it would be her, that she'd left her crew alone at the Rose to deal with the busiest night of the week because she couldn't stand it anymore, not talking to him, being apart from him. Maybe she had even come to her senses and decided she'd been an idiot not to accept his marriage proposal.

He took his sweet time answering the door.

But then it wasn't her, after all.

It was Tabby Ellison, long red hair sleek as a satin sheet, green eyes hard, looking as angry at him as he was with Corrie. "What's going on, Matt? You never call."

He almost shut the door in her face. But instead he made the mistake of trying to be reasonable with her. "We broke up, remember, weeks ago?"

"Of course we didn't."

"Tabby. We did."

"We had a fight. You said some awful things."

Actually, she was the one who'd said awful things. All he'd said was goodbye. He tried that again. "Goodbye, Tabby." And he gently shut the door.

But she was ahead of him. She stuck one of her thousand-dollar shoes in the way. "We have to talk."

"No. We don't. It's over. Done. Move on."

"Matt—"

"Please get your foot out of the way. Now."

To his surprise, she did what he asked her to do.

Matt shut the door and locked it, half-expecting her to start pounding on it and ringing the bell. But she didn't. Faintly, he heard the tapping of her four-inch heels as she went down the front steps.

He heard a car start up and drive away. With a sigh of relief, he went into the living room and dropped to the sofa. He just felt crappy, about Corrie. And about Tabby, too.

Really, what had he been doing the past couple of years with Tabby? Yeah, she was good-looking and intelligent and she ran in the same crowd he'd been raised in. But she was way too much like her BFF, Lianna Mercer, who'd been engaged to his oldest brother, Ash—until Ash had met Tessa Jones and found out what he'd been missing. In the end, a man needed more from a woman than a big trust fund and the right social pedigree. He needed the important things, like laughter and kindness and honest affection. Both Tabby and Lianna were spoiled rich girls, pure and simple.

As he sat and pondered the many differences between Corrie and Tabby Ellison, the doorbell rang again. He stayed where he was. With a little luck, Tabby would give up and go away.

Then his cell rang. He assumed it must be Tabby trying yet another angle. But he dug the phone out of his pocket and looked at the display, just in case.

Corrie. His pulse started racing like he was headed straight for a cardiac arrest.

It rang again. He put it to his ear and tried to sound casual. "Hey. What's up?"

"Where are you?"

"What do you mean? I'm home."

"Then would you mind answering the door?"

It took him a second or two to realize what her question meant. Incredible. He'd fantasized her leaving the Rose on the busiest night of the week just to try and make things up with him. But he'd never actually believed it would happen. He cleared his throat. "It's you…at the door?"

"You were expecting someone else?"

He decided against going into detail on that. "You just surprised me, that's all. Come on in."

"Can't. I didn't bring my key."

"Stay right there…" A minute later, he was flipping the lock and pulling the door wide. She was there, on his porch, in a black pea coat and the sexy purple camisole, tight jeans and high-heeled boots she often wore to the Rose. "Shouldn't you be working?" He asked the question and wished he could call it back. It sounded gruff and critical.

But she didn't get huffy. She only grinned. "Yeah. I should be. But they can manage without me for once. And they can always call if there's an issue. Kira in bed?"

He nodded. "She's been asleep since a little after eight."

She hunched into her pea coat and shivered a little. "You gonna let me in?"

He stepped back. "Absolutely."

She came in and he shut the door and then they just stood there in the foyer, staring at each other.

He stuck his hands in his pockets. "I don't suppose you're here to tell me you've decided to marry me after all?"

"No."

"I was afraid you'd say that."

"I'm here to tell you I miss you and I hope that you'll forgive me soon and we can be…friends again."

"Friends."

"Well, okay." Her mouth quirked on one side in a nervous, hopeful half-smile. "Friends with benefits?"

Another pause as he looked at her and she gazed back at him.

He wanted to reach out and pull her into his arms. He'd been yearning to hold her every minute of every hour since he'd left her at her house the Monday before. But he felt strangely shy. He kept his hands to himself and confessed, "I missed you, too. A lot."

"Oh, Matt. I'm glad."

"Give me your coat."

She took it off and he hung it in the closet. Then he held out his hand. She put hers in it.

They went up the wide stairs side-by-side. And in his room, they made love. It was really good. But then, it always was with Corrie.

Corrine called Aleta early the next morning. "I didn't want you to worry. I stayed the night at Matt's."

"Ah." There was a world of gentle understanding in that

single syllable. "Good enough, then. Thanks for letting me know." In the background, Corrine heard a man's deep voice. Aleta spoke to him. "It's Corrine. She's at Matt's…."

Corrine knew who the man was, but she asked, anyway, "Davis there?"

Aleta spoke into the phone again. "He is. And I have an idea. Why don't you and Matt bring Kira over here for breakfast? I'm making French toast. You know how Kira loves French toast…"

The last thing she wanted was to eat breakfast across the table from Davis Bravo. But then again, she really did need to get over her animosity toward him. Aleta would appreciate that. Plus, he *was* Kira's grandpa and Matt's dad.

Burying the hatchet would be the best thing for all concerned.

Corrine said. "Hold on. I'll ask Matt." The three of them were already in the kitchen. Kira sat at the table sipping a glass of orange juice Matt had poured for her while he fired up his ginormous espresso machine.

He sent her a glance over his shoulder. "Ask me what?"

"Aleta's making French toast. We're invited."

Kira set down her glass and let out a crow of delight. "I *like* French toast!"

Matt must have picked up Corrine's hesitation. "My dad's there, right?" At her nod, he arched a brow. "That okay with you?" She made a face—but she nodded again. "Well, all right then. Tell her we're on our way."

Davis Bravo was almost sixty. Still, like all of his sons, he was a good-looking man, trim and fit. He had a thick head of silver hair and heavy eyebrows that had yet to go gray.

He greeted them at the door, shaking her hand, telling her that it was good to see her. No, she didn't buy it for a second, but she nodded and smiled and said how nice it was to see him, too. He didn't so much as lift a bushy eyebrow at the sight of her snug, low-cut cami, which, along with the rest of her work clothes, was all she'd had to put on that morning after her impromptu decision to go to Matt the night before.

Kira held out her arms to Davis and he scooped her up. "How's my best girl?"

Of course, she told him. In detail. "Yesterday, Daddy took me to my lessons and then we went to have frozen yogurt. I had chocolate. I *like* chocolate. With sprinkles. I *really* like sprinkles." She rattled on about what she'd had for dinner and the movie she'd watched before she went to bed. "And then, in the morning, I woke up and Mommy was there. She had a sleepover with Daddy last night. I bet that was fun."

"I'm sure it was." Davis looked more amused than anything. Corrine figured that maybe he wasn't so self-righteous nowadays, since his wife had left him and he was having to knock himself out trying to get her back, since he'd ended up experiencing a few sleepovers of his own.

"Give Grandpa a kiss," Corrine suggested dryly before her daughter could say more about what a good time she thought her parents must have had last night. Kira planted one of her smackers on his cheek and then reached out for her grandma, who caught her, hugged her and got a big, fat kiss, too.

They went to the kitchen, where the table was set and the coffee was brewed. There was bacon and fresh fruit. Aleta manned Corrine's electric grill and Davis poured them coffee and got milk for Kira.

It was a little weird, Corrine thought, sitting in her own kitchen, having Matt's parents wait on her. Odd, but kind of nice, really. Davis remained on his best behavior through the meal.

Once she'd eaten, Corrine excused herself to clean up and change. When she came back down fresh from the shower in a skirt and sweater, Matt and his parents were still sitting at the table. Kira had moved to her kid-sized table in the corner. She was busy with her crayons, bent over a big piece of construction paper.

"Put on some jeans," Matt said as Corrine went to the counter and poured herself a last cup of coffee.

She turned, leaned against the counter and sipped. "And I should do that why?"

His admiring gaze went over her, head to toe and back again, bringing a slow warmth inside as she remembered the pleasures they'd shared the night before. He said, "We're all going out to the ranch."

And then Davis added, "Please. Join us." He spoke a little stiffly. But he *had* actually extended the invitation. He was definitely trying.

She'd been planning to choose another church from the phone book. But Matt's tender glance and Davis's honest attempt to smooth over old hurts had her rethinking her plan.

And then Kira said, "Look, Mommy. It's our family, all together."

Her daughter was holding up the picture she'd just drawn: a row of stick figures, five of them, all holding hands, each wearing a big, red smile. Kira was the smallest, in the center. Corrine recognized Davis by his bushy black brows. "It's beautiful, baby," she said around a certain tightness in her throat, as Matt and his parents made admiring noises.

"Put it on the 'fridgerator."

"I absolutely will." She turned her gaze to the three sitting at the big table. "I'll just run upstairs and change."

"…When she left us and moved to your house, I started thinking they'd never get back together." Mercy, Luke Bravo's new wife, stood at the window in the sunroom, gazing out through the rain at the gardens behind the ranch house. "But now I'm starting to get the feeling they're working things out."

Corrine stood at her shoulder. "Yeah. I'm betting Aleta will go back to him, probably in the next week or two."

The rain hit the windows and flowed down the glass in a thousand tiny streams. Corrine, Matt, Kira and Matt's parents had barely made it to Bravo Ridge and up the steps of the wide front verandah before it had started coming down.

It hadn't stopped. So they'd spent the rest of the morning and the early afternoon inside, which had been kind of fun. They'd watched a movie in the media room on the giant-screen TV, then had lunch. Davis had played Crazy Eights with Kira for more than an hour.

The sight of them sitting across the coffee table from each other, each deep in concentration over their cards, had Corrine seeing the family resemblance between them. It was there in the identical way they tipped their heads when they were thinking, in their deep-set eyes and strong chins.

Now, while Kira napped, Matt, Luke, Davis and Aleta had driven out to the stables. Luke wanted to show them some new horse he'd bought. Corrine had stayed behind with Mercy, to enjoy a cup of tea and get to know Luke's bride a little.

Mercy, who had thick black hair and eyes to match and clear, smooth olive skin, turned to give Corrine a smile. "I've been to Armadillo Rose a few times. I like it. The music's good, the atmosphere is friendly. I've always had a good time there. I ran into Luke there once, before we started seeing each other." Her black eyes turned dreamy. "We danced…."

It had been quite a shocker, when Mercy and Luke got married, what with the longtime feud between her family and the Bravos—not to mention, her sister Elena turning out to be Davis's daughter.

Mercy spoke again. "It's a big thing, between Luke and me, to do all we can to bring our families together. After years of both sides going at it like the Hatfields and the McCoys, we want it to be different now."

Corrine asked carefully, "How's your dad doing?"

"Not well." Mercy stared out at the rain again. Javier Cabrera's reaction to learning of his wife's betrayal had been a violent one. He *had* attended Mercy's wedding, but no one had seen much of him since. "I mean, he's okay physically, really. But he keeps to himself a lot now. He and my mom are still apart."

Corrine didn't ask if Mercy thought her adoptive parents would ever get back together. She could guess by Mercy's sad expression that the answer would most likely be no.

Mercy forced a smile. "But we'll be inviting my dad to Thanksgiving dinner here at the ranch. And my mom. And of course, Elena will be here. And the whole Bravo family. As I said, the idea is to keep working on everyone, slowly getting them to see that we're all one family now." She chuckled, a wry sound. "It's a big job."

Corrine grinned. "But someone's got to do it."

"That's right. And speaking of family, I hope you and Kira will come, too."

Corrine considered. "Thanksgiving at Bravo Ridge. That would be…different."

Mercy frowned. "You're not telling me you've never been invited before?"

"No, I'm not. Matt's tried for years to get me to come here for holidays with the whole Bravo crew— and he always included my mom in the invitation, too, before she died."

"But you never accepted?"

"No. Kira comes for Thanksgiving every other year, though. She was with me last year, so you can expect her this time."

"Why wouldn't you come, too?"

"Truth?"

"Please."

"Davis has never been my favorite person. It just

wasn't my idea of a good time, coming here for a family get-together, wondering what mean thing he might say to me."

Mercy wore a knowing look. "He's treated you badly?"

"He has. He never did like the idea of me and Matt together. And he hated that I had Kira. He thought it was totally white trash of me to get pregnant without being married—not that he ever wanted me for a daughter-in-law. I'm not up to his standards. Which is fine with me. He's not up to mine, either."

Mercy shook her head. "He tried to come between Luke and me."

"I can't say I'm surprised."

"There's more. He didn't only try to get Luke to dump me. He also tried to get between Ash and Tessa. *And* Gabe and Mary." Ash and Gabe were the other two married Bravo sons. "Tessa told me he really pushed to get Ash to forget about her and stick with his engagement to Lianna Mercer. The story on the street is that Lianna dumped *him*...."

"I never believed that," Corrine said.

"Me neither. And Gabe said that Davis tried to lean on him to stop seeing Mary."

"What *is* his problem?"

Mercy suggested, "Just your average old, rich, white dude?"

They laughed together. Then Corrine admitted, "He does seem to be trying lately, though."

Mercy agreed. "After he got used to the idea that his three oldest sons married the 'wrong' women, he's treated us all decently—even affectionately. Also, I think

Aleta walking out on him has shaken him up some. And really, he loves his children. It's his main redeeming quality. He wants his sons to be happy. Even more than he wants them to marry rich women with connections in the world of big business." She slanted Corrine a smile. "Did you know that Luke and I are having a baby?"

"Aleta told me. Congratulations."

Mercy laid her hand on her softly rounded tummy. "We want to have at least four."

Corrine thought of Kira. "They do change your life in the most amazing ways."

Mercy gazed at her steadily. "Come for Thanksgiving. Please."

Corrine thought about Matt, wondered how things would be going between them by then. And then she reminded herself not to be negative, that it wouldn't hurt her at all to assume the best possible outcome— whatever that might be.

"Say yes," Mercy urged.

"Well, okay, then. Yes. I'll be here."

They stayed at the ranch for dinner that night. And when they all went back to Corrine's, it was after eight.

Kira had her bath and Matt tucked her in. Around nine, Aleta and Davis said good-night and went upstairs together.

Once they were gone, Matt pulled Corrine close. "I thought they'd never leave."

"They're not gone—they're right upstairs."

He kissed the end of her nose. "When *is* she going to move back in with him?"

"Mercy and I were wondering about that, too."

"And?"

"I'm thinking soon. Also, Mercy asked me to Thanksgiving dinner." Corinne paused for effect. "I said I would come."

"You're kidding."

"No, Matt. I'm not. I'll be there."

He studied her face for a second or two. And then he grunted, a satisfied sound. "About damn time." He kissed her, fiercely at first, but then more tenderly. It became one of *those* kisses, the best kind, the kind that go on and on.

When the kiss finally ended, she sighed and rested her head on his shoulder. "I would love to lead you upstairs and take off all your clothes, but…"

He understood. "It's a little crowded around your house lately."

"Mmm-hmm." She stared into the fire, feeling lazy and content, wrapped in his arms, watching the flames leap and dance.

"I had a great time today." He kissed the crown of her head.

"Me, too."

He tipped her chin up, brushed another kiss across her lips, a sweet one, light and quick. "We should spend Sundays together more often. If you married me, we could—"

She punched him lightly on the shoulder. "Give it up."

He caught her face between his big, warm hands. "We didn't really talk about it the other night when you turned me down."

"What's to talk about?" She tried to keep it light.

He wasn't having that. "What have you got against marriage?"

She took his wrists, pushed them away, and she spoke more firmly than before. "We've been through this."

He let go—but he didn't back off. "You're not answering me."

"I've got nothing against marriage. Remember, until about two weeks ago, I was engaged."

"Then what? You resent me for screwing up the thing you had with Bob?"

"Of course not. I told you. If it was right with Bob, I never would have spent the night with you."

"So you don't resent me for ruining the thing you had with Bob and you have no issues with marriage?"

"No, I don't. On both counts. And can we please—"

He cut her off. "Well, all right, then. What have you got against marriage to *me?*"

"I like things the way they are, okay?"

"No, it's not okay. I want to understand what the deal is, what's keeping you from even considering saying yes." He spoke in a gentle tone that belied the determination in his eyes.

She almost asked him why it was suddenly so important to him, the whole marriage thing. But she stopped herself just in time. Asking him why would only encourage him.

He added, "And even if you're going to stick with saying no, I don't see why we can't at least talk it over."

"Matt. Please."

"Please, what?"

"You're just…" She didn't finish. Maybe she'd get lucky and he'd give it up.

Not a chance. "What? I'm just, what?"

"You're just such a total…*man.*"

"And this is bad?"

"Of course not. In a lot of ways, it's terrific."

"But."

"Because you're a man, you don't just talk things over for the sake of a good discussion or to work something out in your own mind."

"So?"

"So when men talk things over, they always have a definite goal they're shooting for. They're always working to get the other person to see the light—which, to a man, means to do what they want the other person to do."

"You think I'm manipulating you."

"Matt. No. I don't. I told you. I think you're trying to convince me to see the light. *Your* light. You're trying to get me to see things your way. And you're wasting your time. There's no point in talking with me about something that isn't going to happen."

"Because I'm a man and men never talk about things that aren't going to happen."

"Right. I mean it. There's no way we're getting married. I'm totally firm on this and no matter what you say, you're not changing my mind."

He was silent. They stared into the fire together for a time. Then he said, "Is it about your dad?"

"Matt, come on."

"Well, is it?"

"I hardly remember him."

"He abandoned you. Just walked out the door and never came back. Are you scared I'm going to do that to you?"

You bet I am. "Please. Seriously. We're not getting married and I'm…" What? She didn't even know how to finish her own sentence. He had her spinning in circles. "Look. Can we just stop talking about it?"

He caught her chin again, made her look at him. "I'm not leaving you, Corrie. I never have and I never will."

"I know that. I…appreciate that so much, the kind of dad you are to our daughter. I know she will always be able to count on you. That's really something. I wish I'd had a dad like you. But marriage? Uh-uh. No way. I want your word that you're going to stop asking me."

"You want my word." His eyes burned into hers.

"That's what I said."

"Why do you need my word? If there's nothing I can do to convince you to change your mind, well, what's the harm in talking about it?"

"Because it's a waste of time."

"Not to me."

"Matt. I mean it. I really do want your word that you'll shut up about marriage."

"Well, too bad. You're not getting it."

Chapter Eight

Matt forced himself to drive home slowly.

When he got there, the house was too damned quiet. He turned on the flat screen in his bedroom, cranked the volume up high. And then he sank to the end of the bed and watched a couple of big brunettes yell at each other on some reality show or other.

At the first commercial break, he changed the channel. Nothing much was on. When he got fed up with surfing, he turned the damn thing off.

The silence, after all that racket, was downright deafening. He tossed the remote toward a chair across the room and fell back onto the bed. It was still unmade after last night. He'd never gotten around to it that morning. And Greta, his housekeeper, had weekends off.

Last night had been good.

All nights with Corrie were good.

He closed his eyes and imagined her naked. It took the edge off his fury with her, at least a little.

The house phone rang. He reached over and grabbed the cordless from the nightstand. "Yeah."

Corrie said, "You still mad at me?"

A smile tried to creep up on him, despite his intention to keep the anger going. "I mowed down five innocent pedestrians on the drive home. It's all your fault."

"At least you kept it under ten."

He couldn't help thinking what a damn fine friend she was. And the best lover he'd ever known. Maybe she was right. Why mess with success? "I'm still mad. But I'll get over it."

"Whew."

"My dad left yet?"

"Nope. He's staying the night. And most likely tomorrow night. And the night after that. Every night your mom will let him, until she's finally ready to go home to him."

"I have an idea—and don't get your defenses up. It has nothing to do with the M-word."

"Umm?" It was a seductive, inviting sound. He could see her, in bed, her eyes low and lazy. The image had him thinking about all the really exciting things he would like to do to her body. She suggested, "I'm listening."

"Stay here, with me."

"Uh, when?"

"Tomorrow night. Every night you feel like getting away from my parents."

"You wouldn't mind?"

"If I minded, I wouldn't have offered."

"Not on work nights, though, right? I'd be disturbing you. I don't get home till two-thirty. Sometimes later."

He imagined her, in the middle of the night, slipping into bed with him, trying not to wake him. The idea pleased him. "Any time is good. No matter how late."

"What about Kira?"

"This is her home, too. Bring her. Or leave her with her grandma. Whatever works on any given night."

"Matt. You sound so…flexible."

"Because I am. Mostly."

"Yeah. You are. You really are." She was smiling. He could hear it in her voice. "I…I think the world of you, Matt."

So why won't you marry me?

He didn't ask. He was done asking. "Tomorrow night, then? The Rose is closed, so you can come for dinner. And bring Kira. I'll have Greta whip us up her famous German meatballs, with Black Forest cake for dessert. Kira loves Black Forest cake…"

"Matt, I…"

He waited. But she said no more. Fair enough. "All right." He spoke in a tone both flat and final. "See you then."

Corrine felt semi-rotten.

Okay, more than semi. Just plain rotten. Totally rotten.

She knew she had hurt Matt, not only by refusing his proposal—twice—but also by not explaining herself.

Except she *had* explained herself. Things were good with them and why take a chance of ruining that?

He wasn't buying her reasoning. He was certain she had deeper, darker reasons for turning him down. And maybe she did.

But really, she saw no point in going into those sad, old, pitiful reasons. She couldn't see how revealing her deepest secrets would help him to accept her decision on this. The way she saw it, digging up old garbage wouldn't do anything but stink up the place.

He would get past this. *They* would get past it. They had a very good thing going and there was no reason to make any big changes. No reason to take scary chances that could end badly. Marriage was a big step. *Too* big a step.

She and Kira got to his place at six the next evening. They ate dinner. They watched TV for an hour. Kira had her bath and Matt tucked her into bed and read to her until she fell asleep.

Corrine went to his bedroom to wait for him. When he joined her, she was sitting on the bed, wearing nothing but a welcoming smile.

He came and stood above her. She looked up at him, at his dear face, at his eyes that were turning smoky-gray with arousal. He said, "You are so damn sexy."

"Thanks."

"I think I should probably lock the door."

"Do it."

He went and turned the privacy lock. Then he returned and stood above her again, looking down at her, his gray gaze hot as the barrel of a smoking gun. "It's good. To have you here."

"Thank you. For inviting me." Her heart had found a slower, deeper rhythm—the rhythm of desire.

"Your eyes are midnight blue right now…" He was already hard for her, the bulge at his zipper more than obvious.

She extended a hand and cupped him through his trousers, hiding her woman's smile when a low groan escaped him. "You have too many clothes on."

"Yeah?"

"Umm-hmm." She stood and went to work on the buttons of his shirt.

He captured her hands. And then her mouth. And then he gathered her into him and kissed her so hard and deep it made her whole body hum with yearning, with that bone-melting need only he could ease.

Then he released her and got out of his clothes. He opened the drawer by the bed and took out a condom, tore off the wrapper and put it on.

"Oh, Matt…" She reached for him.

He grabbed her close. They fell across the waiting sheets, rolling, mouths locked together.

It was wild and good and more than a little rough. She reveled in it—in the roughness and the sheer sexual glory of it—crying out in pleasure when he scraped his teeth along her neck, when he caught her nipple and sucked it hard. He kissed his way down the center of her body, tugging on her navel ring so carefully, with his teeth, then going lower.

All the way. He kissed her there, where she wanted him most. He knew the spot, never had any problem finding it. He found the place and he worked his own special brand of magic there, sucking and teasing, stroking with that wicked tongue of his, until she begged him with wordless, whimpering sounds.

She caught his head, speared her fingers into his thick, spiky hair, and pressed her yearning body hard against his mouth. He didn't stop. He went on and on, tormenting her in the most perfect way. It was his own special revenge against her, she knew. For refusing to accept the ring he had offered.

For keeping herself just a little apart from him. For insisting on protecting that final central part of her life from the possibility of the havoc he could wreak on her—*had* wreaked on her, once upon a time.

He made her suffer in the most glorious way, coaxing her to the brink once, pushing her over. And then waiting, backing off a little, his warm breath soothing her, easing her heat, until he sensed she was ready again. And again. And then again.

After that fourth time he took her all the way to climax and right on through, she was crying out so loud and so desperately, he had to reach up and lay his hand across her mouth, to quiet her a little, to keep her from shouting the house down.

That touch—the simple, gentle pressure of his hand against her lips…

That touch reached down inside her, somehow. It made the tears rise. She let them fall. They trickled back along her temples into her hair. And still, below, he went on kissing her, teasing her, loving her, creating endless, building waves of desire and fulfillment that somehow always became desire all over again.

At last, when she thought she would die from the never-ending pleasure he wrung from her, he lifted his head. She moaned and reached for him, tried to pull him back down, to make him torment her some more.

But he only gazed at her, his gray eyes, silver now as the eyes of a wolf, gleaming at her. His mouth glistened. Her own wetness was smeared on his chin.

And then he pounced, sliding up her body so fast, bringing his wonderful, hard male weight all along the length of her. She felt him, there, the tip already easing in, right where she needed him most. She was open and so wet and oh, so willing.

He slid inside—glided in, so thick and hard. She welcomed him with a hungry moan, accepting him so eagerly, feeling her inner body stretching willingly to have all of him, so deep and so good. She lifted her arms, wrapping him tight. And sliding her legs up so she could hook her feet behind his back.

She offered her mouth and he took it. He took all of her. Everything.

And she gave herself up to him, losing herself in him, in the pleasure he gave her. She surrendered her body fully. With total abandon.

She could afford that. To give him her body, completely.

It was her heart she wouldn't—couldn't—bear to surrender to him. Not again.

Never again.

Corrine went to Matt's after work for the next three nights, climbing into his bed with him in the darkest hours of the early morning. Each night he turned and reached for her, either to make love, or to pull her close in sleep.

All three nights, she left Kira at home with Aleta, who got her up in the morning and took her to school. Friday night—which was Saturday morning by the time she left the Rose, Corrine went back to her own house. She didn't want her daughter waking up every morning without her mom.

She fed Kira breakfast and then took her to Matt's. He urged her to stay. But she had errands to run and piles of laundry that weren't going to wash themselves.

He kissed her before she left, whispered, "Tonight…"

She talked to him at four on his cell.

He said, "Your daughter's been after me. She hasn't forgotten we promised to take her to Chuck E. Cheese's last Sunday, but we went to the ranch instead. She says she does love the Bravo Ridge, but we did promise her. 'And it's not nice to break your promise, Daddy.'"

"Well, we did promise. Actually, *you* promised."

"Yes, I did. And I'm a guy who keeps his promises."

The way he said that had her dreading another go-round on the subject of marriage. He hadn't brought it up since Sunday night. She'd been kind of hoping they were done with that.

He went on, "So what do you say? A thrilling visit to kid heaven in an hour or two? I know you have to work tonight…."

"It's fine. Kid heaven is definitely doable."

"Are my parents at your place?"

"Your mom is."

"Invite her. See if she can get hold of my dad and get

him to come, too. Kira was very specific. She claims we're all supposed to go."

Corrine chuckled. She knew her daughter, who was nothing if not specific when it came to saying what she wanted. "Ten minutes. I'll call you back."

Corrine invited Aleta and Aleta called Davis. He was there in a limo in fifteen minutes, flat. They took the limo to Matt's, where he and Kira joined them. The driver dropped them off at Chuck E. Cheese's. They had pizza and soft drinks. Davis bought Kira way more tokens than he should have. She rode all the little-kid rides and played all the little-kid games. The adults took turns following her around.

When not currently on duty watching Kira, they sat at the table, drinking too many soft drinks, smiling and not talking a whole lot. At Chuck E. Cheese's, the music and the games were kept at one level: loud. It was hardly the kind of place for adult conversation.

They got back to Matt's at a little after seven. Kira was beat. Matt got her bath going. She hugged everyone goodbye, complete with the usual loud, happy kisses.

Matt came back downstairs just as they were going out the door. He caught her hand. The look in his eye said it all: *After work?* She nodded and pulled her fingers free, feeling a little awkward, there at the door, with Matt's mom and dad waiting.

Which was probably beyond silly. Aleta and Davis had to know that she and Matt were lovers now. She was hardly ever home anymore, since she spent most of her nights with him.

Still…

She turned toward the limo waiting at the curb and saw Davis's gaze kind of slide away—clearly, he'd noticed the silent exchange. And she felt a surge of resentment so powerful she had to consciously stop herself from baring her teeth and growling at him. She just knew he had to be thinking that she wasn't good enough for one of his precious sons.

He'd probably have a stroke if he knew that Matt had not only been sleeping with her again, he'd been after her to marry him....

Corrine drew her fury up short. She followed Davis and Aleta back to the limo and ducked inside feeling a little ashamed of herself.

Yes, there was a time when Davis had looked down on her, had considered her unworthy of Matt and had made his opinion of her all too hurtfully clear. But times do change. And Matt's dad had been exceptionally decent and civil toward her the past few weeks—truthfully, he'd been treating her well enough for years now. It was just that memories of his early behavior toward her died hard.

Sometimes even eating your words won't make them go away, her mom used to say. *Better not to say them in the first place.*

Well, Davis Bravo *had* said them. Maybe he regretted that now. But he was going to have to be really nice to her for a very long time before she didn't find herself wanting to slap him silly every time he looked at her.

Corrine slipped into Matt's bed at a little before three Sunday morning. He didn't wake but reached for her in his sleep. She cuddled in close. In the morning, he got up and fed Kira so Corrine could sleep till noon.

Sunday afternoon, the three of them went to the latest Disney movie. And Sunday night, after Kira was tucked in bed, Corrine and Matt made long, slow, sweet love.

Monday, Matt left for BravoCorp at eight and Kira went to kindergarten in the morning, with lessons later. Once the lessons were out of the way, Corrine took her home to put the finishing touches on the pilgrim costume for the Thanksgiving play that Wednesday. Kira modeled the costume for Matt that evening after dinner, complete with the slightly lopsided construction-paper pilgrim hat she'd made herself a couple of weeks before.

"You look great, sweetheart," Matt told her. "Very authentic."

She wrinkled up her little nose. "Authentic?"

"Like the real thing. A real pilgrim lady."

"Oh, yes! That's right!" Kira beamed. "I'm authentic, that's what I am."

After that, everything was authentic. Her bath toys. The book she wanted Matt to read her when it was time for bed. "Daddy. Read me this one. It's authentic."

When Corrine came in to kiss her good-night, she announced, "Mom. Give me a real kiss, an *authentic* kiss…"

Corrine gave her just that, complete with the preferred loud, smacking sound.

Later, in bed, Matt told her he was going to Los Angeles for a week to firm up a solar energy project with a distant Bravo cousin.

She snuggled in closer to him. "BravoCorp's in solar

energy? I thought you guys were all about property development and big oil."

"We are. But land development projects are pretty much on hold, what with the current economy. We've got a high-end housing development in progress up I-10, not far from Boerne, called Bravo River Homes. We'll carry through on that. It's a sustainable-resource project and we're proud of it. And oil is…well, it's always going to be a big part of what BravoCorp is about. But we're in wind energy already—and we've invested in solar, too. We want to move into more green energy solutions. Taking on a bigger solar project is the next step."

"When will you go?"

"A week from today for five days."

"So you'll be here for Kira's play—and Thanksgiving?"

"Absolutely."

She was already missing him, which only proved how far gone she was getting over him. Matt had been on a lot of business trips in the years since she'd had his child. She'd never missed him in advance of his leaving before. That was something a woman in love did—and she was not in love with Matt. No way. Uh-uh. "So you'll be gone Monday through Friday…"

"Right. Back a week from Friday, in the afternoon. Gabe and Ash will go, too." Gabe was BravoCorp's lawyer and Ash was the company's CEO. "Ash is bringing Tessa…" She felt his lips at her temple in a tender, brushing kiss.

She stopped him before he could say it. "Sorry, I can't go with you."

He went still beside her. Too still. Tense-still. "Did I ask you to go?"

"You were going to."

"You have no way of knowing that."

"Matt."

He made a sound, a grunt that told her he was listening, at least.

She said, each word precise, "Were you about to ask me to go?"

He pulled away. She felt the bed shift as he reached over and turned on the lamp he'd switched off a few minutes before. When he faced her again, he braced up on an elbow and glared down at her. "You said no without a damn nanosecond of hesitation. You didn't even consider the idea. You didn't even give me a chance to ask you to go."

"So then. You *were* going to ask me?"

"It's not the point, Corrie."

"It *was* the point about ninety seconds ago."

He glared some more but didn't immediately reply. And that gave her time to admit to herself that she was being a total bitch about this.

She said with real regret, "Look. I'm sorry. You're right. I did jump to the conclusion that you would ask me. And then I said no without giving it a second thought."

His expression relaxed. "So, then. How about it?"

She cast about for a delicate way to turn him down. "Oh, Matt…"

His jaw stiffened all over again. "Why not?"

"Kira needs—"

"—someone to love her and look after her while we're gone. My mom will be glad to do both."

"Of course she would. But there's the Rose. Matt, you know I have to work. In the bar business, the boss really needs to be there. Skipping a night now and then is one thing. But three nights in a row…uh-uh. I don't think so."

He put up his hand, palm flat. She raised hers to meet it. They twined their fingers together. "How long since you had a little time off?"

"Saturday before last. I took the night off. I came here, to see you."

"One night does not a vacation make."

"It's just…not a good idea right now." The excuse sounded totally weak, and she knew it.

He opened his fingers and pulled his hand free of hers. "When *will* it be a good time?"

"Matt. Come on." She pushed him over onto his back and rose up to lean over him. "Let it be."

"I know it's not smart to bring up the M-word with you, but you're married to that bar, you know that?"

She kissed his chin—though it was firmly set against her. "That's not true."

"So then, when will you let me take you away somewhere romantic, somewhere with palm trees and balmy beaches?"

"We'll see, okay?"

"That's a limp-ass excuse for a 'never' if I ever heard one."

"Kiss me, Matt."

"You're just trying to distract me with sex."

She slid a hand down beneath the sheet and encircled him. "Kiss me…."

He groaned. "Guess what? It's working."

* * *

Wednesday evening was Kira's school play.

Davis had his driver take them in the limousine. They all agreed Kira was a standout. She played a pilgrim wife and had two lines: "We are here to gain freedom from religious oppression." And, "Thank you, oh great Sachem, Massasoit, for sharing your corn."

She spoke those lines out loud and clear, without a stumble, even though they contained several big words. And she looked adorable in her pilgrim dress and crooked hat.

Afterward, while they shared cookies and punch with the other students and their families, Kira solemnly explained that her tall black hat wasn't really the *authentic* kind of hat a pilgrim wife would wear.

"But I like the men's hats better, so I made one. And Miss Bell let me wear it." She was frowning. "Why did the men have better hats than the women?"

Davis scooped her up in his arms. "Because that was four hundred years ago when men ran the world. Things have changed since then." He put on a mournful frown. "It's very sad." And then he winked at her.

Kira laughed. "Oh, Grandpa. You're so funny."

Corrine watched the exchange, feeling all warm and fuzzy inside. Davis did love her daughter and that mattered a lot. She would try to remember that when she found herself resenting him for what he'd said and done in the past.

They dropped Matt off at his house on the way home. He sent her a look as he got out of the limo. She gave him a nod, meaning she would be over after she finished at the Rose for the night. He kissed Kira and shut the door and the limo rolled on up the street.

She sat back in the plush seat, getting that sentimental feeling again. No matter how long their second chance at romance lasted, it was something special to be with a guy who could understand you with just a shared look.

She smiled to herself. Must be the season. She was feeling thankful for everything that evening.

The next day was Thanksgiving and the Rose was closed for the holiday. They all headed out to Bravo Ridge together—Aleta, Kira, Matt and Corrine. Davis was already there. He'd gone ahead, first thing in the morning.

Eight of Davis and Aleta's nine children showed up for the party. Even the brooding loner and ex-con, Jericho. Only Travis, seventh-born—after Jericho and before Abilene—didn't make it. Gabe brought his wife, Mary. And Ash came with his bride, Tessa. Gabe's stepdaughter, Ginny, seven months old with shiny baby curls and the cutest dimples you ever saw, was there, too. And Mary's former stepmother, Ida, as well. Matt whispered to Corrine that Gabe thought the world of Ida and that since Gabe and Mary had gotten together, Ida had become like a member of the Bravo family.

Luz Cabrera was there. According to Matt, she was in her late forties. She looked amazing—a stunning woman, with a fine, full figure and thick brown hair. Elena attended, too. She looked like her mother. But the shape of her face and the strong chin? All Bravo.

Elena hung out with Caleb a lot. Matt said that Elena and Caleb had become close a few months before, after they found out that they were half brother and sister. A year younger than Matt, Caleb was BravoCorp's top sales rep. He drove fast cars and dated a lot of women. Back in October, Matt had told her that Caleb was going out with Ash's former fiancée, Lianna Mercer. When Corrine had asked Matt why, he had shrugged and replied, "Because Caleb never could resist a pretty face."

Now, in a whisper, she asked him, "So why didn't he bring Lianna to Thanksgiving?"

Matt sent her a look. "He got smart—finally—and called it off. Now he's going out with Emily Gray, a BravoCorp executive."

"Is that a good idea, dating someone at work?"

"I don't believe he's thinking with his brain, actually."

Corrine stifled a laugh. "I see."

"Truth is, we're all figuring he'll end up with his housekeeper, Irina. Have you met her?"

"Uh-uh."

"She's very quiet. Serious. Takes great care of him. She's Victor Lukovic's cousin—you know, the line-backer for the Dallas Cowboys?"

Corrine nodded. "Caleb's friend from college."

"That's him."

She was still thinking about Lianna. "You said Caleb got smart and dumped Lianna. You don't like her much, huh?"

"Well, it's just that she happens to be a complete bitch."

"Hmm. And her best friend is Tabby Ellison, right?"

He scowled. "I know where you're going with this. Don't."

"So Tabby's a nicer woman than Lianna, then?" The question kind of hung in the air between them.

Finally, he shrugged. "Tabby? Who's Tabby?" He wrapped an arm around her and nuzzled her hair.

Corrine laughed. "Excellent answer."

Javier Cabrera was a no-show, which everyone had more or less expected.

Corrine got to know Tessa and Mary a little. She liked them both. Tessa was tall and sturdily built, with pale blond hair. It only took one look in her eyes to know she had a tender heart. Mary was a calm person, honest and direct. Corrine could respect the Bravos a lot more now she knew the kind of women the three oldest sons had married. Tessa, Mary and Mercy were all good women. Strong and level-headed, loving. And kind.

The afternoon and evening passed like most good times—swiftly, in a warm glow of family together-ness, of laughter and lively conversation. Corrine chatted with Mercy, and with Abilene and Zoe, the Bravo daughters. Abilene was pursuing a masters degree in architecture. Zoe, the baby of the family, had been to and dropped out of three colleges. She laughed and said she had no idea what she would do with her life.

It was after nine and Kira had fallen asleep on the couch in the living room when Corrine started thinking that maybe they ought to head back into town. Matt had gone off an hour and a half before with a couple of his brothers—presumably to the game room for a few hands of poker or a little nine ball.

The game room was at the back of the house, not far from the sun room, accessed by the central ground-floor hallway. Halfway along it, Corrine heard voices from beyond the open door to one of the many rooms that lined the wide hallway.

Without really considering that she was eavesdropping, she slowed her steps.

"I know that you and your husband have been living apart." A woman's voice, soft and musical, with a pleading note. Corrine knew whose voice it was: Luz Cabrera's.

"Davis put you up to this." It was Aleta's voice, aloof and proud, her slight drawl more pronounced than usual. She was upset. Really upset. She always sounded like the queen of Texas when she got angry.

"No. I swear to you. I know because Mercy told me. Not from Davis. Your husband and I avoid each other. We're both happy with that. I asked to speak with you because *I* want you to know—"

"I have no idea what you could possibly say that would make any difference to me, one way or the other." Aleta's voice quivered with emotion.

Corrine considered rushing in there and rescuing Matt's mom from a situation that had to be terrible for her.

But then again, Aleta had a right to fight her own battles. Plus, Luz had seemed like such a nice woman— the whole adultery issue aside.

Luz spoke again, but so softly that Corrine couldn't make out the words. As she stood frozen with indecision, someone in the room shut the door.

Now Corrine heard the voices very faintly. And that decided her. This was not her fight.

She moved on down the hall, past that closed door,

to tell Matt that they really did need to get going. And she ignored the sinking feeling in her stomach, the one that promised some terrible disaster was about to occur.

Chapter Nine

But nothing out of the ordinary happened. Corrine found Matt. They returned to the front of the house to get their sleeping daughter and say their goodbyes.

Aleta appeared as they were going. She looked perfectly fine, composed and unruffled. She said that Davis had promised he would take her back to Corrine's a little later that night.

Corrine longed to grab her and hug her and demand, *Are you really all right? What happened between you and Luz?*

But she did no such thing. Matt picked up their daughter and settled her on his shoulder. They thanked Luke and Mercy for a wonderful Thanksgiving.

Mercy pulled Corrine close in a hug. "So then, Christmas dinner?"

Corrine laughed. "As far as I know, yes. I'll call you…."

"Good."

At Matt's house, they put Kira to bed and she and Matt went to his room. They took a long bath together in his giant bathtub with the massaging jets. They made love.

It wasn't until he'd turned out the light and they were both on the brink of sleep that she said into the darkness, "Something went on between your mom and Luz tonight."

For a moment, he said nothing. He was lying very still. She began to think he must already be asleep.

But then he shifted toward the edge of the bed. The lamp popped on. "What?"

"Something happened between—"

"Wait. Got that part. But *what* happened, exactly?"

So she told him what she'd heard in the hallway. "I was certain there would be big trouble."

"Certain, how?"

"It was something in your mom's voice. If she'd had a weapon, Luz would've been toast."

"But whatever it was, they worked it out, right? They must have. My mom seemed fine as we were leaving."

Corrine nodded. "Yeah. She did. If I hadn't heard their voices in that room, I never would have guessed that anything went on."

"So whatever they said to each other, it wasn't the end of the world."

"Guess not."

He reached for the lamp. The room faded into darkness. He scooted close and gathered her into his arms.

"I had a good time tonight," she whispered.

She felt his lips in her hair. "I'm glad."

Corrine rested her head on his chest and let his strong, steady heartbeat lull her to sleep.

However, as it turned out, something serious *had* happened between Aleta and Luz.

Corrine learned what early Friday evening, after Matt dropped her off at her house to get ready for work that night. He took Kira back to his place, because the plan was that Corrine would return to Matt's after the Rose closed up for the night.

She found Aleta's suitcases lined up against the wall in the entry hall.

Matt's mom was waiting for her on the sofa in the living room. Aleta smiled at her. A tender smile. The smile of a mother, of a really good friend. "I know you have to get to work. But I was hoping we could talk for a minute or two?"

Crazy, but Corrine felt tears scald the back of her throat. She swallowed them down. "Going back to Davis, huh?"

Aleta patted the sofa cushion next to her. "Come over here. Sit by me."

Corrine dropped her purse on a chair and went to sit beside her. "Well?"

Aleta wrapped an arm around her. "Thank you."

"No need for thanks."

"Maybe not. But I do need for you to know that being here, with you and Kira, has been the loveliest time for me—which is really something, if you think about it. Before you took me in, I felt almost as though my life was over. I had no idea how to sort it all out. But you gave me what I needed—time and a warm, loving place, in a truly difficult phase of my life, Corrine. And I am so grateful."

"Whatever I gave you…" Corrine's throat was so tight, it almost hurt to speak. "…you gave back to me, a thousand times."

"How sweet of you to say so."

"I don't know about sweet. It's just the truth. And speaking of the truth? Last night I overheard you and Luz talking…" Corrine explained what little she'd heard. "And then someone shut the door."

"That was me. I suddenly realized anyone might go by and hear us."

"Well, you were right. Someone did go by. I wanted to bust that door down and save you—but then I realized you would probably rather fight your own battles."

"Yes, I would. But you've been worried." Aleta squeezed her shoulder.

"Yeah. You seemed okay when we said goodbye last night. But I was still…you know, concerned."

"Put your mind at ease. Luz only told me what I needed to hear. That my husband loves me. That Davis didn't hide the truth from me for more than twenty years. That he never knew Elena was his. Luz swore to me she didn't tell him. And she's certain he never figured it out. She reminded me that if he had known, she would have heard from him about it. At the very least, he would have insisted on giving her money. He never did. She said that men can be blind when seeing the truth will only cause pain and trouble. Somehow, that made total sense to me."

"She…eased your mind, then?"

"She did, yes. And she apologized to me for all the harm and hurt she's caused. She said she doesn't believe her husband will ever return to her, that what they shared is broken, forever. That it can never be fixed. She also said that if at least Davis and I can work things out, some of her burden will be eased. That's how she put it, her 'burden.'"

"The poor woman."

"I realized I *like* her," Aleta said wonderingly. "I think she's a good person who made a couple of very bad choices. And she's certainly paying a terrible price for what she did. Yes, she and Elena have reached a kind of truce. But they're not close anymore. That has to be hell for her—that her own daughter doesn't trust her. And Luz does love Javier. It broke my heart to see her face when she said his name. To love a man that much and to know you'll never hold him close again."

Corrine saw the truth shining in Aleta's eyes. "She's helped you forgive Davis."

"That's right. She has. Her taking me aside and insisting I hear her out… It was the final nudge I needed to realize how much I love my husband, to see that I do, absolutely, want our marriage back. Because I…" Aleta whipped a tissue from the box on the coffee table and dabbed at her suddenly brimming eyes.

Corrine's eyes were wet, too, by then. She took a tissue of her own. "You've doubted him, doubted his love for you."

Aleta made a low, sad little sound. "I did wonder if it was all a lie, our life together. I wondered if maybe he had married me for my wealth and social standing more than for myself."

"But you're past that now."

Aleta swiped at her eyes, dabbed at her nose. "I am. Yes. Davis can be pigheaded and overbearing and judgmental and so annoyingly superior."

Corrine chuckled through the tears. "Tell me about it."

"But I love him."

"Oh, I know you do."

"And during the past couple of months since I've moved out, as he's pursued me relentlessly, he's finally succeeded in convincing me that he loves me, too."

At his house, Matt hung out with Kira until eight. Then came the bedtime rituals—her bath, her story, a good-night kiss. He turned out her light and closed her door and went to his room, where he took off his shoes and stretched out on the bed.

When he woke up it was ten after two. He went downstairs to wait for Corrie.

At five of three, he heard her car pull up in front. He headed for the foyer and opened the door for her so she wouldn't have to fiddle with her key. She came up the steps in her usual pea coat, tight jeans and cami, a dark blue one this time, that matched her eyes.

He grabbed her arm and pulled her into the warmth of the house, shut the door with his foot and kissed her hello.

"Long night?" he asked when he lifted his head and got a closer look at the shadows under those beautiful eyes.

She leaned her head on his shoulder. "You'd better

believe it. We had three fights break out. That's a record, I'm pretty sure. Jealous men. Angry women. They all seemed to be at the Rose last night."

"You want a drink or something?"

"If I never see another drink, it's going to be too soon."

"A bath, then?"

"Now you're talkin'."

So he ran a bath for her, poured in the bubble-making stuff she liked and didn't wait for her to invite him before climbing in with her.

"Come here," he said, once he'd settled in among the bubbles.

She floated around so she could lean back against him. He gathered her in and pressed his cheek to the top of her head, thinking that his house always felt more comfortable, more like home, when she was in it.

She said, "Your mom has moved back in with your dad. When you dropped me off last night, she was waiting to tell me, with her bags all packed."

He wasn't particularly surprised. "It was bound to happen."

She sighed and rested her arms on top of his, which were wrapped around her waist. "Yeah." Idly, she stroked his forearms. Her touch felt so good. She said, "I'm gonna miss her, though."

He kissed her temple. "I know."

"And I need to find a new sitter for work nights."

"No rush." He cupped her breasts. They felt just right in his hands. "Kira can stay with me in the meantime."

"Too bad next week you're gone."

He dipped his head and brushed a kiss on the moist,

sweet-smelling curve at the base of her neck. "We can find someone, don't worry."

"I'm not worried." She sent him a soft smile over her shoulder. Her skin was pink from the steam that rose off the water, her hair curling into corkscrews at her nape, her body smooth and slick and tempting against his. He wished he'd brought a condom into the bathroom with them. She said, "Your mom told me that she and Davis would love to have her at their place any time I need a sitter."

He considered the fact that he would have to leave the bathroom to get protection. Inconvenient, to say the least.

She laughed, a low, very sexy sound. "Did you hear what I just said?"

"Every word. And if my mom will take Kira, no problem then." He caught her nipples between his fingers.

She made a tender little moaning sound. "If you keep doing that, I'll be too breathless to tell you what actually happened between your mother and Luz."

Reluctantly, he wrapped his arms around her waist again. "Tell me." She did. When she finished, he said, "Well, it's good to hear she's finally realized the obvious."

"What do you mean, the obvious? Why wouldn't she have doubts? He had an *affair,* Matt."

"A long time ago, an affair she's known about since right after it happened—and haven't we been through this all before?"

She huffed a little. "Yes, we have. Though apparently you didn't hear what I said then."

"Oh, yeah. I heard you, loud and clear. And I agree. He screwed up. Royally. And he's one lucky bastard he didn't lose her for good, that she's finally willing to forgive him. But still…"

"What?"

"It's just so obvious he loves her. That he's always loved her."

"To you, maybe. Apparently, not to her—and come on, think about it. Mercy told me your dad tried to mess things up between her and Luke. *And* between Ash and Tessa. *And* Gabe and Mary. Okay, maybe his interference between Luke and Mercy was more about the whole family feud thing than about Mercy person-ally. But when he tried to get Ash to forget Tessa and Gabe to dump Mary, well, there's only one reason why he would do that. He didn't think they were good enough for his sons. And then there was the way he treated me…"

Matt pulled her closer. "Come on. Do we have to go into all that again?" And then he had a sinking feeling. He took her shoulders and floated her around so he could see her eyes. "Has my dad done something?"

She looked confused. "Something…?"

"You know, has he said anything that hurt you, has he—?"

"Matt." She lifted a bubble-covered hand and laid her fingers against his lips. "No. Truly, in the past four years or so, your dad has been a perfect gentleman to me." She let her hand drop beneath the water again.

He wiped the froth of bubbles from his mouth. "You're sure?"

"Of course, I'm sure. I have no issues with your father—well, not recently, anyway. I haven't forgotten the way he treated me in the past. But as of now, he's always civil to me and he loves Kira. I could hardly ask for more from him. And that wasn't my point. Will you let me make my point?"

"Come back here first."

"Oh, all right. She turned to rest against him again. The water buoyed her, so he wrapped his arms around her and she settled in good and close. "You listening?" she demanded.

"I am."

"My point was that your dad wanted his sons to marry up, the way he did, that he married your mother because she had money and connections."

"Uh-uh. He married my mother because he loves her."

"But he wanted a wife who knew the 'right' people, a wife with a fat bank account."

"So? He got what he wanted. Love *and* a rich wife. Is that so bad?"

"The question is would he have loved her if she was a poor nobody? That's been bothering her for years, maybe since the beginning of their life together. She *knows* him. He's ambitious—grasping, even. She couldn't help but wonder if he loved *her* or what she offered him by being a Randall and an heiress. And then he went and screwed around on her. To her, that was proof positive that he'd never really loved her, and *that* has been eating at her for all these years."

"I see," he said, though he really didn't. The whole issue was too convoluted, the logic much too feminine and emotionally complex, for him to ever fully understand. So he cut to the chase. "But now, after talking with Luz, she's somehow finally been convinced that my dad does love her."

"Exactly. Luz made her see that your dad hadn't been keeping a giant-sized secret from her for all these years, that he really never did know that Elena was his, that when he confessed the affair twenty-plus years ago, he was telling her everything, hiding nothing. Also, since your mom left him in September, your dad has never given up on trying to get her back. He's proved to her that he really, truly wants her for herself."

"Well." He smoothed her damp hair away from her ear so he could kiss it. "Sounds good to me."

"Yeah. It's a happy ending. I love me a happy ending."

He licked the side of her neck. "I've got a happy ending for you."

She floated over to her stomach, slick and quick as a mermaid. And then her fingers found him, wrapped around him. He loved it when she did that. "Tell me all about it," she whispered.

"Better yet. I'll show you...."

Corrine loved every moment of that Thanksgiving weekend. They spent Saturday together, driving Kira to her lessons, sharing dinner, the three of them, like any regular, ordinary family. Then Corrine went off to work.

Matt waited up for her. They made love, and then slept holding each other close. In the morning, he made lattes for the two of them and hot chocolate for Kira; Corrine cooked pancakes. The day went by way too fast.

In the blink of an eye it was nighttime. Since Matt

was leaving before dawn the next morning, she and Kira kissed him goodbye at a little after seven.

He held Corrine close, there at the door, and whispered, "I'll miss you. I'll call you. Every night."

She suddenly wanted to cry. As if he were going away for years or something, instead of just till the end of the week. So she kissed him, holding on tight, pressing her lips to his so hard, letting the kiss go deeper than was probably acceptable given that Kira was standing right there watching.

"Boy," Kira exclaimed when they finally pulled apart, "that was a loooonnnng one!"

Matt scooped her up and hugged her hard. "Be good for Mommy." He gave her a kiss, too, her favorite kind—a loud, enthusiastic smacker on her plump little cheek.

At home, Corrine sent Kira off to take her bath. She turned on the fire and sat in the living room, wishing Aleta had stayed just a day or two more, feeling sad and lonely when there was nothing, really, to be lonely about.

And trying not to start obsessing over her like-clock-work period that was three days late.

Chapter Ten

The next day, Corrine made several calls and finally found a sitter with good references who could start Wednesday night. That left Tuesday not covered. So she called Aleta, who said she'd be glad to take Kira Tuesday night and even get her to school Wednesday morning.

Corrine was all set on the sitter front. But no period yet. She checked often Monday. Nothing.

Just a fluke, she told herself. Even the most regular of women can go off-cycle now and then.

Especially if she's pregnant…

No. Stop. She refused to think that way. Getting all tied in knots over scary possibilities would only made things worse. Stress, after all, could definitely alter her cycle. The more worried she got, the later she would be.

So, then. No more checking. And no more worrying.

It would come in the next day or two. She was absolutely certain of it.

Matt called Monday night. He talked about his second cousin, Jonas, and Jonas's wife, a Texan named Emma. Jonas was über-rich, with a dark past, Matt said. "But he's happy now, with Emma and their kids and his stepsister, Mandy." Jonas's mother had adopted Mandy not long before her death. "Mandy's ten now," he said. "Really talented. Plays four instruments. Can you believe it?"

"Amazing," she said absently, trying not to think about her period and all the trouble it was going to cause if...

No. She stopped herself. Seriously. Not going there.

Matt kept talking. "I was wondering if we ought to consider getting Kira started with an instrument—but then, five is maybe a little young, huh?"

"Um."

"Corrie? You all right?"

"Yes. Of course. Fine."

"You seem preoccupied."

"No." She lied like a rug. "Not at all. Tell me how the solar deal is going."

He did. She took special care to make interested noises whenever he paused for a breath.

When he asked how things were going there, she told him about the new sitter and then gave the phone to Kira, who chattered away as usual, sharing every last detail of her life since she'd left his house the night before.

"Daddy wants to say 'bye." Kira gave her back the phone.

He said he would call tomorrow and then he was gone.

Corrine put her daughter to bed. After that, the house

was way too quiet. She spent an hour checking the invitation list for the annual Armadillo Rose Christmas party, which she always held on the Friday before Christmas Eve. The list included regular customers and her suppliers and their dates, as well as any over-twenty-one family members of her staff.

She added a few names to the list and then e-mailed it to Lauren Evans, a longtime friend who ran a stationery business out of her home. Corrine had already approved the invitation design Lauren had come up with. Lauren would print the cards, address the envelopes and get them in the mail within the next few days.

By the time Corrine sent the list to Lauren, it was after ten. She knew she wouldn't be going to sleep any time soon. So she called a girlfriend she hadn't seen since the wine-tasting a month before—the night she betrayed Bob with Matt.

Time does fly when you're having a hot affair with the father of your child. Naturally her friend, Nona, asked how Bob was.

Corrine set her straight. "Bob's no longer in the picture."

"Get *out* of here. You broke up?"

"That's right."

"But you said he was perfect for you."

"Yeah, well. It turned out not so much."

"Want to talk about it?"

"I'd rather poke both my eyes out with a burning stick."

"Eeeuu. Corrine, honey. You need a drink." Nona's solution to most problems involved a drink. Or several.

"I'm fine. Seriously. How have *you* been?"

Nona was only too happy to tell her. At length and in detail.

After she said goodbye to Nona, Corrine started thinking about her period again. To get that off her mind, she went into the kitchen and baked some brownies.

The tempting chocolate smell of brownies in the oven had always soothed her. Her mom used to make brownies all the time….

Baby, buy a home test, her mom would say if she were there. *Take the damn thing. You can't deal with a problem until you're sure there really is one.*

Corrine ate seven brownies and went to bed long after midnight feeling like a total pig. A possibly pregnant one.

Matt called at ten the next morning, after Corrine took Kira to school. "Because I said I would call every day," he told her. "And I'll be in meetings till seven, at least. And by then, it'll be nine in Texas and you'll be at the Rose."

They talked for maybe ten minutes. She was careful to keep her mind off the pregnancy test she needed to take and on the conversation. He never once asked her if something was bothering her. When she hung up, she congratulated herself on not worrying him unnecessarily.

Later that day, she went out for groceries. She didn't buy a home test. Inside her head, her mom's voice chided her for putting off the inevitable.

"Except it's *not* inevitable," she said under her breath as she waited in the checkout line. "Just a couple days more. I'm sure it will come…"

"What's that?" asked the elderly woman in line ahead

of her. "You young people ought to learn to speak up if you want to be heard."

"Oops. Sorry. Just talking to myself." She gave the old lady a sheepish smile, which the woman did not return.

At the Rose that night she felt vaguely sick to her stomach through her whole shift. But it wasn't morning sickness, she was certain. Just tension and worry, that was all.

Wednesday, as soon as she got Kira off to school, she headed for the Rose. Three of her bartenders joined her to help decorate the place for Christmas. They draped garland from the ceiling fixtures, put up a big tree and covered it with shiny balls, strung white lights all over the place. She left them to finish up when it was time to get Kira from school.

Marilyn Rios, the new sitter, came at five. Corrine spent a half hour giving instructions and showing her where everything was. She was a freshman at San Antonio Community College, getting her gen-eds out of the way, she said, planning to go into dentistry.

Corrine left the house at six, a little earlier than usual. When she got home at 2:30 Thursday morning, Marilyn said that Matt had called. He'd left a message that he would call at 10:00 a.m. Texas time.

By ten that morning, she'd dropped Kira off at school and stopped at a Walgreens to pick up the test she had finally admitted she needed to take. She bought three of them, so she could be extra sure. She talked to Matt before taking one because if she ended up having something to tell him, she didn't want to be tempted to burst out with it on the phone.

He said he would be home around noon Friday. She told him she couldn't wait.

And then she went into the bathroom and did what needed doing.

The result was no surprise. She was pregnant with Matt's baby. Again.

She cast her gaze toward heaven. "What now, Mom?"

No answer. Only silence. Where are the spirits of the dead when you need them most?

She'd bought those other two tests, though. Maybe one of them would give her a better answer. An hour later, she took a second one. Positive. And another after that. Positive again.

Three out of three. She supposed that made it official.

Corrine threw up twice that day. She wondered how this could be happening. Again. She tried to imagine how she was going to tell Matt that he was going to be a dad for the second time. Trying to imagine that brought on flashes of guilt so stunning and fierce, she almost threw up all over again. She'd been totally irresponsible on about a gazillion levels. Betraying poor Bob. And doing it without contraception.

And then, the next morning, she could have—*should* have—gone straight to Plan B.

Matt had even suggested she do that.

And she'd blown him off. She'd been so confident of her damn clockwork cycle. She'd practiced what amounted to the rhythm method and it hadn't worked.

What was that old joke?

What do you call couples who practice the rhythm method?

Mommy and Daddy.

Dumb. Beyond dumb. Stupid to the nth degree.

Somehow she got through the day.

She went to work that evening thinking she'd only stay a few hours, leave early, go home and go to bed before three in the morning for once. Surely her situation would look brighter after a full night's sleep.

The Rose was pretty busy, but no more so than most Thursday nights. All of her people showed up for work. By nine, she was thinking she could probably duck out within the next hour, leaving her head bartender in charge.

Too bad she didn't leave right away. At nine-thirty, as she helped clear a table, someone tapped her on the shoulder.

She turned around and almost dropped her tray of dirty glasses. "Uh. Tabby. Hey."

Matt's former girlfriend was looking sleek and gorgeous as always. Tabby's red hair fell straight and thick and smooth to her model-skinny shoulders. And on her perfect oval of a face there was not a single freckle.

It just wasn't fair. A girl should either be gorgeous *or* disgustingly rich. Tabby was both.

"I'm at the end of my rope, Corrine. I *have* to talk to you."

This did not sound good. Corrine desperately tried to think of a gentle way to refuse. Nothing came to mind. And Tabby really did look upset.

Still, Corrine made a stab at ending what was bound to be an unpleasant conversation before it could get started. "Really, Tabby. I don't see what I could do to—"

"Please! Just a few minutes. Just a little of your time."

Bleakly, knowing she would live to regret this decision, Corrine handed her tray to the nearest busman. "Come on," she shouted to be heard over the music. "To my office..." Corrine plowed through the crowd, moving fast, half hoping that maybe Tabby, in her four-inch Jimmy Choos, wouldn't be able to keep up.

But when she went through the door to the storage rooms in back, Matt's old girlfriend was right behind her. Tabby's heels tap-tapped across the concrete floor as she followed Corrine to the office.

Once there, Corrine gestured the other woman in ahead of her and indicated the chair opposite the desk. Tabby paused to inspect the seat, after which, with an expression of mild distaste, she lowered her designer-clad butt into it.

Corrine's frustration and annoyance with Matt's ex-girlfriend spiked. Okay, her office was a mess and the extra chair was kind of dusty. But Tabby could save the snotty facial expressions. Especially considering that she'd shown up here begging Corrine to give her a minute or two.

"It's about Matt." Tabby sighed. Heavily. A tear spilled over her lower lid and tracked its way down her perfect cheek.

Corrine folded her arms and perched on the corner of her desk. "Tabby, seriously. I really don't see how I can possibly help you with—"

"Oh, but you can! Of course, you can. Matt *likes* you. I know you're good friends with him, which is really kind of weird if you think about it, but still. It's the way it is."

"Tabby—"

"You're his best friend and that's why I know that if anyone can reach him, it would have to be you. Because, Corrine, he won't see me." A second tear dribbled down in the path of the first. And another after that. They were sliding down her other cheek, too. She whipped a tissue from her huge purse and dabbed her eyes with it. It was strange, watching Tabby Ellison cry. Her nose didn't even turn red. And her makeup didn't smear, either. "He won't even *talk* to me. I go to his house and he tells me it's over between us when it's *not* over. How can it be over? I don't *want* it to be over." She leaned forward in the chair, glaring at Corrine, expecting her to have all the answers—the *right* answers, meaning the ones that Tabby wanted to hear.

Corrine cleared her throat and suggested carefully. "Well, I guess maybe *he* wants it to be over."

"What are you telling me? Of course he doesn't. Not really. Not deep down. I came here because I want you to tell me how to get through to him. I want you—I *need* you—to help me."

"Tabby—"

"Actually, I was thinking if you *talked* to him, if you tried to get him to see reason and realize that he's just being ridiculous, the way he's avoiding me."

It was too much. It was all just too much. "Tabby, all right. I'll tell him that you came to see me."

"You will?" Those gorgeous green eyes went wide. A gusty sigh of relief shuddered through her.

"I will," Corrine repeated. "But I don't have any idea why you would want me to talk to him for you."

"But…but I *told* you why. You're his best friend."

Corrine stood. "I'm also his lover. I've been sleeping with him since the first week of November. If anyone should talk to him about you, I'm guessing you're really not going to want it to be me."

Tabby's mouth dropped open. She snapped it shut. "You're joking."

"Nope. I'm sorry, but you've pushed me into a corner here. I seriously saw no way out but the truth."

"B-but, you're engaged to a *minister!*"

"Not anymore. Not since I started having sex with Matt again."

Tabby pressed her slim hands to her wet cheeks. "No. It can't be. You're lying."

"Nope. Sorry. It's the truth. And now I guess you can see why I'm not the one to put in a good word for you with him."

Tabby shot upright, her face suddenly almost as red as her hair. "You cheap little two-faced bitch." Her hand shot out.

Corrine caught her wrist before it connected. "Get out of my bar. Now. And please don't come back."

Tabby tossed her red hair and held her chin high. "I will be talking to my father. And *he* will be talking to Davis Bravo—in fact, no. Wait. I'll talk to Davis myself. I've known him and the Bravo family since I was a child. You can believe he won't like what you've been up to."

Corrine spoke gently. "Whatever you got, you go ahead and you bring it."

"Let go of my wrist."

Corrine spread her fingers wide. Tabby jerked her arm away. Corrine commanded, "Out."

Perfect nose tipped toward the water-stained acoustic-tile ceiling, Tabby went. As soon as she cleared the doorway, Corrine swung the door shut and turned the lock.

Then she picked up her phone and called Little Joe, her head of security.

"Hey, boss. Whut up?"

"A gorgeous redhead just left my office. Five-eight, pink top, tight black skirt. Giant purse and high-dollar shoes. Very hot. Make sure she leaves the Rose and doesn't come back."

"You got it."

Corrine disconnected the call and sank to the edge of her desk. Maybe she shouldn't have been so blunt with poor Tabby. And though Davis already knew what was going on with her and Matt, she really wasn't looking forward to learning that he'd gotten an earful about it from the jealous daughter of one of his country club pals.

She knew what her mom would say: *Baby, look on the bright side. Tabby Ellison won't be coming around asking you to help her out with Matt again.*

"That's right, Mom. Got any advice on how to tell Matt I'm pregnant? Again?"

There was only silence from the Great Beyond.

When Matt got off the BravoCorp jet at Stinson Airport on Friday, it was ten past noon.

He rode home in the limo the office had waiting and stayed there just long enough to haul his suitcase in and changed into chinos and a button-down sport shirt. He pulled on a jacket, got behind the wheel of his Lexus and headed for Corrie's.

Timing-wise, he figured he had it about right. Kira had three dance lessons in a row after school. Corrie should have dropped her off at the studio by now. And, if he was lucky, gone on home.

When he turned onto her street, her car was there, in the driveway, just as he'd hoped. He eased the Lexus in next to it and raced up the front walk.

She must have heard him pull in because the front door swung open as he raised his hand to knock.

He drank in the welcome sight of her in old sweats, with her shining face scrubbed clean of makeup. "You look amazing."

"I look like crap." Her gaze kind of slid away and he wondered if something was bothering her.

He said, "I've waited all week to see you naked."

She grinned then. Slowly. He loved that grin of hers. He must have imagined the anxious look of a moment before.

She wasn't anxious now. "Maybe you should come in first. My neighbors aren't real big on nudity."

He didn't have to be told twice. He shot over her threshold and grabbed her in his arms. As he kissed her, she swung the door shut with an outstretched hand.

He considered whether he should undress her right there at the door—or scoop her up and carry her to her room.

So many choices. All of them good.

"How was your trip?" She eased his jacket off his shoulders. It fell to the floor with a soft plopping sound.

"Profitable." He got the hem of her sweatshirt, pulled it up and off. "What's this?"

"Sports bra."

"It's in my way."

"Can't have that." She slithered it over her head and dropped it to the floor next to his coat.

He brushed a hand against her breast. "So pretty…"

"You always say that."

"Only because it's true." He scooped her up then, tight against his chest, and turned for the stairs.

In her bedroom, he dropped to the bed, taking her with him. She ended up on his lap, where she rocked back and forth, her lips locked to his and her tongue in his mouth.

But not for long.

She had plans. She slid to the side, grabbed his shirt and ripped it wide. Buttons went flying. She pushed it down his arms.

He shrugged out of it as she was whipping his belt off and away with a slick, hot whisper of sound. He yanked his zipper open and shoved down the chinos, boxer briefs along with them, shucking shoes and socks at the same time. She got rid of those sweatpants.

And that was it. They were both naked. They fell on each other, rolling, laughing, moaning.

He was so hard for her it hurt. He settled between her soft thighs, positioned his aching hardness at the wet, pink core of her—and caught himself just in time. With a few muttered swear words, he reached for the drawer where she kept the condoms, had one out and on in a few seconds—which was too long, as far as he was concerned.

He sank into her heat. She enfolded him, moaning his name.

Corrine dropped back on the pillow, panting. "Oh, my, yes…" She turned her head to look at Matt.

He smiled at her. "It's good to be home."

She rolled over and rested her head on his chest. He stroked her tangled hair and she listened to his heartbeat, swift and hard. Then gradually slowing…

He said, "I almost messed up again. With the condom?"

Oh, great. Contraception. Such an important subject. One she should have thought about more seriously back when it would have done some good.

She considered opening her mouth and saying it, "Not a problem. I'm already pregnant."

But she didn't. In the end, all she said was, "Um…"

He went on, "I'm thinking we should look into some other method. If we don't, we're bound to slip up again, like we did in November. And like six years ago."

"Um."

"That would be beyond it, huh? You'd think we'd have learned our lesson by now."

"Yeah. You would think."

"So what do you say? The pill, maybe?"

"I'll talk to my doctor." Well. It was true, as far as it went. She would be talking to her doctor, all right. When she went for her first prenatal visit.

"Sounds good." He sounded lazy and content.

She needed to cut the bull, and she knew it. She

opened her mouth to give him the news. What came out was, "So, are you seriously in solar now?"

He chuckled. The sound was a low, manly rumble under her ear. "You bet your beautiful ass we are."

She realized the subject was changed. And she was way too relieved about that. "You're pleased with this deal, then?"

"*I* am, yeah."

"Meaning somebody else isn't?"

"You know my dad. He's kind of old school. But he comes around, gradually. He was all for the wind energy project we got into with Jonas's group last spring. But he gets nervous when there's too much progress, too fast."

"But it's happening anyway?"

Matt shrugged. She felt the movement beneath her cheek. He said, "It's a good deal and he's given it the okay. That's what matters."

Talking about Davis brought Tabby to mind—Tabby and her threats. She wondered with some dread if the crap would hit the fan when Tabby went crying to Matt's dad. At the very least, it was going to be embarrassing. And just when Corrine had more or less made peace with Davis…

Matt squeezed her shoulder. "Everything all right with you?"

I'm pregnant and your old girlfriend called me a cheap two-faced bitch. But other than that…

Corrine sighed. She knew she had to tell him—about all of it. Tabby and the stick turning blue. All three sticks, as a matter of fact.

"Corrie?"

Reluctantly, she peeled herself off the front of him and sat up. Folding her legs in front, yoga-style, she grabbed her pillow and hugged it, seeking a comfort she didn't find.

He sat up, too, dragging himself against the head-board, frowning now. "What's the matter?"

"Tabby came to see me at the Rose last night."

"What the hell? Why?"

"She had some idea that I could help her 'get through to you'—you know, since I'm your best friend and all. She wanted me to convince you that you're being an idiot, that deep in your heart you know she's the woman for you."

"Damn it, Corrie. I'm so sorry she did that. And I swear to you it's over with her."

"I believe you. Too bad *she* doesn't."

"I'll talk to her. I'll make it beyond clear that she and I are done and that she'd better not get near you again if she knows what's good for her."

"I don't think anything you say will get through to her. That is one determined woman."

"I'll get through. Watch." The words were a dark rumble. "And I promise you, there's nothing going on with her and me. I ended it with her just like I told you I did, weeks before that first night, when we had the wine, in November." He looked so worried that she might think he was cheating on her.

She didn't. He had his flaws, but he was no cheater. "Matt. Come on. It's okay. I know you're finished with her."

"Good."

"And I also know that it's totally your call, if you talk to her, what you say to her. But I think we'd all be better off if you just kept clear of her. Way clear. Going up against her is only going to fan the flames. She's a mean girl—a mean girl with a mission. That's the scariest kind."

"She had no damn right to bother you."

"Like I said. Your call. But you ought to know her well enough by now to realize there's not a thing you can do, short of deadly force, to make her knock it off."

"It's not right."

Corrine could see there was no talking him out of it. "You should know the rest."

"The rest? What else did she do?"

"Not her, me. I told her I probably wasn't the one to make you 'come to your senses' and admit you're in love with her, since you and I are lovers and we've been having sex together since early November."

He let out a surprised bark of laughter. "You're serious. You said that?"

"I did."

He grabbed her close to him and kissed her, hard. "That's my girl."

"She got really mad then. Before I ordered her out, she said she would go to Davis about it."

"I will deal with her, Corrie." His voice was hard as a slab of granite.

Corrine grabbed her pillow again. "Okay. Now I feel like a total snitch."

He reached out and dragged her back against him. His arms felt so good and strong around her—and so did the kiss he pressed to her temple. "What else were you going to do? Keep your month shut and let me find out from my dad that she went crying to him? She wants to pull crap like that, fine. It's a free country. And there are consequences."

Corrine didn't like the way he said the word, "consequences," so dangerous and low.

However, it *was* a free country and he had the right to confront his ex. If Corrine had wanted to keep him from doing that, she should have kept her mouth shut.

She was on a roll with the revelations. Seriously, what better time than the present to tell him about the new baby? Let him start getting used to the idea that there would be another kid.

"Matt."

He tipped up her chin and kissed her lips. A lovely, soft, brushing kiss. "Yeah?"

"There's something I need you to know...."

Chapter Eleven

"Tell me." He kissed her again.

She kissed him back, pulling him over on top of her. It felt so good. She didn't want to stop.

But he lifted away and captured her gaze. "What?"

And she totally wimped out. "I'm...so glad you're home."

His eyes held hers, so tender. So...happy. "That's what I like to hear." And he lowered his mouth to hers once more.

They made love again. And then it was time to go get Kira.

Sunday night, she silently vowed. She would do it then, after Kira was in bed. When it was just the two of them, with the whole night ahead of them and no interruptions.

* * *

That evening, while Corrie was at the Rose, Matt went to Tabby's place. Tabby wasn't home—which he probably should have expected given that it was Friday night.

He called her cell.

She answered on the second ring. "Matt? Oh, God. Matt…"

"Where are you?" Probably some club. He heard music and chatter, loud, in the background.

"It's so amazing to hear your voice," she cooed. And then she caught herself. Her tone turned sulky. "I shouldn't forgive you. You've been terrible to me."

"We need to talk."

"I…yes. We do. I know we do. Do you…I mean, now?"

"Yeah. Now. How 'bout my place? It's quiet and no one will bother us."

"Hold on." She must have hit the mute button. The background noise went silent. He waited. And then the party sounds were back. So was she. "Lianna says I shouldn't." So she was out clubbing with Lianna Mercer. He wasn't surprised. They were two of a kind. "Lianna says I should make you suffer the way you've made me suffer."

"My place. Half an hour."

"Oh, Matt…"

"Are you coming or not?"

"Yes. All right. Half an hour. I'll be there."

Matt took his time driving home. No need to hurry. Tabby never got anywhere on time. She was always having to change her clothes—again. Or freshen her makeup. Or make a few calls.

An hour and a half after he called her, she finally arrived.

"Matt." She breathed his name on a quivering sigh and swayed toward him—catching herself at the last minute with an anguished little moan and drawing herself up tall. "Oh, I'm such a fool. I can't believe I almost threw myself into your arms."

Lucky for her she'd stopped herself. Because he'd had zero intention of catching her.

He stepped back. "Come on in."

She wore a low-cut party dress and a shawl across her shoulders. With a small, injured "Humph," of sound, she drew the shawl closer and followed him in. "I'll have a cran-tini." She waved her hand toward the wet bar in the corner as she settled herself in the center of the sofa. "And then, if you're very nice, I'll let you come and sit by me."

He ignored her drink order and took a chair across from her, with the coffee table ottoman reassuringly between them. Had she always been so obnoxious? He wanted to believe she hadn't. It would make him feel marginally better about the fact that he'd dated her.

Because, really, there were a lot of nicer women around who might have been willing to go out with him. He could have chosen one of them.

Then again, Tabby had always looked good on his arm. And she knew everybody he knew. And though she'd probably believed they were headed for the altar, he'd known he would never marry her. In fact, being with Tabby had worked out great for him in a lot of ways. Yeah, he'd had to put up with her chronic lateness, her constant posing and her lousy personality. But once she was out of his sight, he never thought twice about her until the next time he needed a date for some party or business event.

That had been convenient for him—dating someone he could forget about until the next time he needed her. Convenient, and completely unlike the way Corrie made him feel, which was wild and dangerous and…hungry. To hold her. To talk to her. To touch her all over. Even during all the years when they were strictly hands-off, he'd thought about Corrie often and looked forward to the next time he would see her.

"Well?" Tabby crossed her pretty legs and fiddled with her sparkly shawl. "If you're not going to get me a drink, the least you can do is *say* something."

"Last night you went to Armadillo Rose."

Her expression went from snotty to tragic in under a second. "All right. I understand now. What did that little—?"

He put up a hand. "If you call Corrie any names, I guarantee that you won't like what I do next."

Tabby subsided into a furious pout. "I just don't get what you see in her, that's all."

"She's smart, she's got a big heart, she's sexy as they come. She's a fine mother. She's got a great sense of humor. She's hardworking. She'll do anything for a friend. Oh, and she's beautiful. Does that answer your question?"

"I'm sure you feel, because of the child, that you have to defend her."

"I don't feel anything of the sort."

"She's…not like us."

"And that's a bad thing?"

"She has no…social skills. She'll say anything. She's not the least concerned with another person's feelings."

And you are? "You're dead wrong."

"How can you be so blind about her? She…she told me right out that she was sleeping with you again."

"Why not? She is. I can't tell you how happy I am about that."

"What about that minister she was supposed to be marrying? What happened to *him?*"

"She realized it wasn't going to work out and she gave him his ring back. Simple and direct. I like that in a woman. I like it a lot."

There was huffing. And a tear or two. Tabby swiped them away dramatically with the back of her hand and stood. "I should have listened to Lianna. She was right. You refuse to see what a mistake you're making. And you only got me over here to torture me. I've had enough."

"Do not go near Corrie again. Do *not* go running to your dad—or mine. Stay out of my life, Tabby. I don't want anything more to do with you."

She shot around the end of the ottoman. "I can't believe how cruel you can be."

He rose and blocked her path. "Say you understand me. Say you'll stay away from Corrie."

She huffed and quivered. But then, at last, she muttered, "I understand, okay? I won't go near that—"

"Do. Not. Say. It." He made each word a sentence.

There was sniffing and a great, shuddering shake of that red head. "Fine. You don't have to worry. I won't go near your precious Corrie ever again. Now step aside, please."

He did. She stormed past him.

The house shook when she slammed the door.

Corrine got home the next morning at three and found Matt waiting for her.

"I gave your sitter a big tip and sent her home early. Hope that's okay…"

All Corrine needed was one look at his face. "You talked to Tabby."

"I did."

"And?"

He described the encounter, ending with, "So at least she promised she'll leave you alone."

"You think she meant it?"

"If she lied, I may have to buy a shotgun."

"Don't even joke about guns, please."

He hooked an arm around her waist and hauled her close. "You don't think my talking to her did any good."

"Did I say that?"

"You didn't have to. You've got that look—the one that says you don't approve, but you're keeping your mouth shut about it."

"Well, it's done now."

"…as in, 'can we stop talking about it?'"

"Since when did you start reading minds? You're becoming downright…sensitive."

"Why does that sound like a dig?" He put on a wounded expression.

She bracketed his face with her hands. "No way it's a dig. I like a little sensitivity in a man."

"But would you have sex with a sensitive man?"

She tried not to laugh. "Somehow, it always comes back to sex with you."

"I may be sensitive, but I'm still a guy."

She pulled his face down and kissed him. "Let's go to bed."

"Best offer I've had all night."

She took his hand and led him up the stairs.

Later, she lay awake beside him, feeling guilty about the baby, dreading telling him, knowing she had to. She'd so been here before. And she had sworn she would never end up here again.

Never say never, baby, her mom would say.

Funny how platitudes tend to be more annoying than helpful.

Saturday seemed to fly by. Even the busy night at the Rose went past at the speed of light.

Suddenly it was Sunday morning. After breakfast, they took Kira out to the ranch. Mercy, who was a large-animal vet and often on-call weekends, was working that day. Corrine missed seeing her.

Davis and Aleta were there, though. They seemed really happy together. Corrine was happy *for* them. Davis treated Corrine kindly and never gave her so much as a strange look. Maybe Tabby really was keeping her promise to Matt and not running to Davis after all.

While Kira napped, the men went out to the stables. Aleta and Corrine stayed in and had tea in the sunroom.

They chatted about everyday things: the weather, the coming holidays, how big Kira was getting.

"Mercy says she invited you for Christmas. You're coming, I hope."

She thought about the baby, wondered, as she was always wondering lately, what would happen with Matt when she told him. Still, it seemed rude to keep hedging. "I'll be here."

"At last. After all these years. It's about time."

"Yeah. You're right. I guess it is."

"Next Sunday, we decorate the ranch house. It's a family tradition. You're invited for that, too."

"It sounds like fun."

"That means yes?"

"Absolutely. I'd love to come. And Kira is real big on decorating. We'll put up the tree at my house next Saturday, around noon? Join us?"

Aleta beamed. "You know I will."

Corrine longed to confide in Matt's mom. She knew Aleta would be kind and understanding if she told her about the baby. Matt's mom would listen sympathetically and pull her into a hug and promise her that everything would work out. And Aleta could be trusted. She would keep the secret if Corrine asked her to, for as long as Corrine wanted it kept—at least, she would keep it from Matt.

She just might feel she had to tell Davis, though, since she had a real thing about absolute honesty between husband and wife. Davis was the last person Corrine wanted told. True, eventually, he would have to know. But certainly not before Matt.

And anyway, much as she longed for comfort, it wouldn't be right to tell Matt's mom first. Matt deserved to be told before she let anyone else in the family know.

They had dinner at the ranch and went back to Matt's afterward. There was the usual: Kira's bath time and then her story. Matt tucked her in.

Corrine waited for him in his private sitting room, off his bedroom. When he joined her, he locked the door to the hallway, for privacy. Which they were going to need, though not for the reason he probably assumed.

She was sitting on the sofa. He crossed the room and joined her, wrapping an arm around her, pulling her near. She cuddled her head in the crook of his shoulder, dread squirming like a live thing in her stomach.

He rubbed her arm, a fond gesture. "Your daughter loves you. She told me to tell you."

Her heart was pounding so hard. A thousand excuses tumbled through her brain: Why ruin a beautiful Sunday? She was only a month pregnant; he didn't need to know yet. He didn't need to know for weeks. A month. Two...

At least she could wait until after the holidays, let them all share Christmas together before throwing the baby news into the mix.

"You want to watch some TV?" He reached for the remote.

She knew then, with absolute certainty, that if she let him turn on the television, she wouldn't tell him tonight. She'd allow herself to put it off.

And it was wrong to put it off, to lie to him with silence. She was having another baby and he deserved to know.

"Wait!" She grabbed his arm.

He turned his head slowly to look at her. "Corrie? What the—?"

"We, um, we have to talk." Her throat clutched up, tight as a square knot tied by an Eagle Scout. And then, suddenly, she was coughing, just hacking away like a two-pack-a-day smoker.

Matt pounded her on the back. "You want water?"

She hacked some more, nodding frantically, gesturing in the general direction of the mini-bar in the corner. He left her long enough to fill a glass.

And then he was back. He took her hand, closed her fingers around the glass. By then, the coughing had slowed down a little. She sipped. It helped. The soothing wetness slid down her raw throat and the clutching eased.

"Thanks."

"More?"

"No. I'm okay now." At least on the choking front. She set the glass on the coffee table.

He sat down beside her again. "You're sure?"

She pressed her hand to her chest and sucked in a slow breath. Her throat had relaxed at least. Her stomach was suddenly churning, but it was manageable. She felt reasonably certain she wasn't going to end up running to the bathroom. "I'm okay." She took another deep breath. "I think."

He laid his hand on her back, a comforting touch. "You said you wanted to talk…."

She made herself face him, made herself look straight in those cloud-gray eyes. No words seemed right. She whispered, "Oh, God. I just don't know how to tell you. I don't even know how to begin."

He took a wild guess. And nailed it. "You're pregnant again."

Chapter Twelve

*P*regnant. The word seemed to ricochet inside Matt's head.

Pregnant.

She was. He knew it by the look on her face. By the fact that she didn't instantly shake her head, or laugh, or tell him he was wrong, wrong, wrong.

Just to make certain, he asked, "Am I right?"

She gave a fierce little nod.

He still couldn't quite believe it. "You're sure?"

"I took three tests. I'll be glad to take another if you want to see for yourself."

He shook his head. It wasn't that he needed proof. It was just that he was having a little trouble processing, getting past that first shock. It had been the same way the last time—only worse.

A whole lot worse. Maybe having kids was like most things. Really hard the first time, but it got easier. At least for the man.

They were staring at each other. Neither of them seemed to know what to say next.

So he took a bold crack at it. "That first night, when we slipped up…?"

"That would be the one."

Of course, it was. They'd been careful after that.

She should have done the Plan B thing. He'd told her to do it. But she wouldn't listen. Damn it, he longed to say I told you so. He didn't, though. He kept his mouth shut. It would only get them into an argument. He could see that by the defensive jut of her chin, by the way she had her lips pressed together into a thin line.

She accused, "I know what you're thinking, Matt."

"No, you don't."

"Yes, I do. You're thinking that you said I should get the morning-after pill. That I told you it wasn't necessary. You're thinking, look what a mess I got us into."

Clearly, she knew him much too well. He tried to think of something brilliant and soothing to say to her. Nothing came.

And his silence wasn't working for her. She kept after him. "Go ahead. Lie to me. Tell me that's not what you're thinking."

He gave in and confessed it. "Partly, okay?"

"What does that mean, partly?"

"It means, yes. It's partly what I'm thinking."

"Well, go ahead, then. Don't hold back. Say it. Just say 'I told you so' and let's get that over with."

"You'll only get mad."

"The hell I will."

"You're mad already."

"Say it, damn you."

Wearily, he made his confession. "Fine, Corrie. I told you so."

"I knew it. I knew you were thinking that." She wrapped her arms around herself and rocked back and forth. "And you're right, you're so right. I totally messed up. It's all my fault…."

"Corrie…"

Still rocking, she stuck out her palm at him, the talk-to-the-hand gesture. "No. Don't try to soften the blow. Just say it. It's all my fault."

"But it's not."

At least she stopped rocking and put her hand down. She said softly, miserably, "It is."

"We both get full credit, you know that. True, you didn't listen when I suggested the morning-after pill. But we both forgot the condom. It was a joint act of irresponsibility. So don't play the martyr on me. It's not your style."

"You really feel that way?" She tried to hide it, but he heard the hope in her voice.

He spoke slowly and clearly. "I do. I honestly do."

She blew out a hard breath and sagged back against the sofa. "Well. At least you know. And it's a bonus that you're not blaming me."

"Yeah. It's good that I know. And I'm glad that you told me right away." He took her hand and felt somewhat encouraged when she didn't jerk away. "It's not the end of the world."

"I know. And *you* should know, in case you were wondering, that I'm keeping it."

"Damn right you are."

She almost smiled. "Well, at least we're agreed on that."

Now he was getting over the shock, he could see that it wasn't a bad thing at all. It was good. In more ways than one. Now, she would have to see that they really should get married.

He suggested, reasonably, "We can certainly afford another child."

She gave him a sad little shrug. "Yeah. There's that. It could be worse. We could be broke. It costs so much to raise a kid these days...."

"And we're not getting any younger."

She laughed, which he took as a good sign. "I don't know what that has to do with anything, but, yeah. True."

"I just mean, people get older. The years go by."

"Yeah, they do."

"Kira would love a new brother or sister."

"You're right. She would. And a lucky thing, too. Because she's getting one."

He could see it all now, so clearly. He wanted her to see it, too. "It's going to be fine. We'll get married. Right away. We can fly to Vegas—or maybe you want a big wedding. That's fine. Either way's okay with me and we—"

"Matt."

He knew by the way she said his name that there was a problem. "Yeah?"

"I, um, no. Not marriage. I didn't say marriage."

He took a long moment to let that—the sheer idiocy of it—sink in. "No marriage."

"That's right—and come on. Don't look at me like you want to strangle me. We've been through this."

Calm and reasonable, he told himself. He was staying calm. He was speaking reasonably. Softly, he reminded her of the patently obvious. "Everything's changed now."

"No, everything hasn't. I'm pregnant, yes. But I was pregnant before. We didn't get married then."

"It's…different now."

"How so?"

Reasonable. He repeated the word slowly in his mind. He would remain reasonable. He would not, under any circumstances, lose his cool about this. He tried for humor. "Well, I mean, one child without a wedding is bad enough. Two is downright embarrassing."

She didn't laugh. After a minute, she said flatly, "You want to marry me to save yourself from embarrassment."

"Corrie, come on. It was a joke."

"Not a very funny one."

"Sorry. I'm doing my best here. And what I'm really trying to say is…" What *was* he trying to say? "…I'm older, you're older. We're both ready to do the right thing now."

"But *you* weren't, back then."

He studied her for a long, hard minute, wondering what was going through that female mind of hers. Finally, he asked, "Is that your problem? You're still mad at me for something I did six years ago?"

"I'm not mad."

Bull. "Oh, yeah. You are. You're mad. I *said* I would marry you then."

"That's right. You did. And you were scared to death I would actually take you up on it."

"What? Are we rewriting history now? The way I remember it, you came to me and told me you were pregnant, right after which you announced that you didn't expect me to marry you. But still, I said I would."

"But you didn't *want* to."

"The bottom line is, I *would* have married you."

She let out a snort of disgust. "I saw the look on your face when I told you. You were terrified and you felt trapped."

"But I was willing. That's the point. I would have done it."

"And then resented me for the rest of your life. No way. I wasn't going for that. I'm worth more than that."

"So that's it, then? That's your problem, that's why you've turned me down—what?—three times in the past month? You're out for revenge because I didn't marry you six years ago."

"Revenge? What are you talking about? Of course, I'm not out for revenge."

"The hell you're not—and you want me to beg you now, is that it? To fall all over myself trying to make up for what I didn't do back when?"

"No, no, I—"

"You want me on my damn knees?"

"Matt…"

He shoved the coffee table out of the way and sank to his knees at her feet. "All right. So here I am. On my knees. Please, Corrie. Marry me. I'm begging you. I'm at your feet, the way you've always wanted me to be."

She wanted to slap him. He could see it, see the heat and fury in her eyes. She had her hands clenched tightly together, to keep from striking out, and she spoke in a voice that was as low as it was deadly. "I swear. You are just like your father, after all. Pig-headed. Blind. And the answer is still no. No, I won't marry you. And if you just *have* to know why, it's because…" She let the sentence trail away. Shutting her eyes, she breathed in through her nose. "Will you please get up off your knees?"

By then, he was starting to feel a little ashamed of himself. Okay, he *had* behaved somewhat like the old man. He'd let his frustration get the better of him, said some things he shouldn't have. "Look, Corrie, I—"

She was shaking her head. "Just get up. I mean it. Just please, get up."

So he got up. And then he stood there, above her, looking down into her upturned face, feeling like an idiot, embarrassed at his own behavior and, at the same time, pissed as hell with her, for being every bit as pig-headed and obstinate as he was. For dredging up the way he'd blown it in the past instead of dealing with him as the man he was now.

She threw up both hands. "Don't just stand there staring at me."

So okay. He would sit down. He backed to a club chair across from her and lowered himself into it. "All right. I'm sitting down. Finish your sentence."

"What sentence?"

"You won't marry me because…?"

"Oh. That."

"Yeah, that."

"You're serious? You really want to know?"

"How many damn times do I have to ask?"

"Fine. All right. You want to know, I'll tell you." She dragged in another deep breath, this time with her mouth open, like someone about to dive into very deep water. And then she said on a hard exhalation, "Because I love you."

Love. The word echoed inside his head.

He got the picture then. Crystal clear. He saw it all, and what he saw wasn't good.

Love.

He'd never actually said the word, had he?

And that was a really big screwup. As big, in its own way, as forgetting the condom that night a month before.

Why the hell hadn't he said it?

He wasn't exactly sure.

But he *was* sure that trying to correct himself now wasn't going to be a viable option.

She had more to say. "I love you." She told him again, slowly, with painful precision. "I've always loved you, since that first night you walked into my bar and turned my whole life upside down. Loved you—though I've never been fool enough to even admit it to myself until tonight. I love you." Those blue eyes filled with tears. She blinked them away. "And you *don't* love me. And you know what? I can live with that. It's just…how it is. How it's always been with us. We can be friends. We can be lovers—oh, Matt. You are the best friend. And an amazing lover. And you are such a good dad to our daughter. I know you'll be good with our second child, too. But this—this marriage thing. Uh-uh. Forget it. I don't want a husband who's just doing the right thing. I want someone who loves me as much as I love him—all the way and over the moon. I won't spend my life wondering if my husband is going to wake up one day and realize I'm not the one for him, the way my dad did to my mother."

He'd sat still for most of what she said. But that last, he couldn't let stand. "I'm not your dad. Don't even hint that I am."

She swiped the persistent tears away. He wanted to reach for her, to comfort her. But he knew she wouldn't allow him that. She said, "Of course you're not—but I mean, seriously. What's the point in us getting married? Why take the chance on that kind of hurt and destruction? Our daughter is doing just fine the way things are. I'm sure our second child will, too."

What she said made his anger rise again. Because he did believe in marriage. And he wanted it now—was ready for it now. With her. "It would be better for them, for the kids, if we were married. You know that."

"No. I don't. Marriage isn't always the answer."

"It is for us."

"Uh-uh. I don't think so."

How does a man make a blind woman see? "I'm not going to leave you, Corrie—not you or our kids. I never have, have I?"

Her lower lip quivered. "No. No, you haven't."

"And I never will. Isn't that enough?"

"No. It's not."

He felt like a drowning man. Flailing. Sinking. By

then, he was willing to try just about anything. Even the thing that he already knew wasn't going to work. "Listen, I know you're not going to believe it if I say it now. But the thing is, I do lov—"

"Don't." She stopped him, just as he'd known she would. Her eyes were dry now, her expression determined. She rose. "It's enough, all right? Enough for tonight. You know about the baby. And I've said way more than I should have about…all the rest."

He stood, too. He gave it one more try. "Corrie, come on. We can talk this out."

She shook her head. "I am so tired of talking. I need to go home now. I need to…throw up and take a bath." She sighed, a heavy, exhausted sound that made him want to grab her and shake her, to shout at her to wake up. To make her see that this was important and she was fading away on him. She added, "And about Kira? I'd rather let her sleep. Can you take her to school tomorrow? I'll pick her up, as usual."

"Just like that, you're walking out on me?"

"I'm not walking out. I'm going home."

"You're walking out and you know damn well you are. You've laid the big love bomb on me, put me in my place as just another oblivious, insensitive, selfish guy. Like my father. Like *yours*. And now you're done. You're out of here."

"Good night, Matt."

What more could he say—given that she was through listening? He dropped into the chair again. She left without another word.

Chapter Thirteen

"Mommy, where's Daddy?" Kira asked Thursday morning at breakfast.

Corrine's chest hurt—as if her heart were all swollen up in there, cramped against the walls of her ribs. She answered with a calmness she didn't feel. "At his house, I suppose. Or maybe at his work."

She hadn't seen him since she'd left him Sunday night. He hadn't called her—and she hadn't called him. They were in a kind of holding pattern. A holding pattern that felt way too much like the one they'd gone into after the *first* time she told him she was having his baby.

Things weren't working out with them—and yet, they had a daughter. And another child on the way. Saturday morning she would be seeing him whether she wanted to or not, at least for a few minutes when she took Kira to him.

And speaking of Saturday, she'd invited Matt's mom to come and help decorate the tree that day. She needed to call Aleta and tell her it wasn't happening. Corrine didn't want to do the tree without Kira, who would be with Matt. And what about the big Deck-the-Halls party on Sunday at the ranch? Matt would probably take Kira for that. He'd taken her every year up until now….

Corrine would have to tell Aleta that she wouldn't be at the ranch Sunday. Aleta was no fool. She would have questions. Corrine hadn't decided what, exactly, to say to her.

It was so strange. Like going through all the pain and awkwardness of getting a divorce, when you'd never been married in the first place….

"Mommy, did you *hear* me?"

Corrine focused on her daughter. "I'm sorry, baby. What did you say?"

"I said, I like it when we all stay in the same house, so that we're all together. Me, you and Daddy, too. Maybe Daddy could come over tonight? He could stay with me while you're working."

"Not tonight, honey. But you'll see him Saturday, just like you always do."

Kira frowned, but she didn't argue. She picked up her spoon and finished her oatmeal.

Corrine found herself considering trying to explain to her daughter that she and Matt were on the outs. But no. That was only guilt talking. It was nothing a five year old needed to hear. The thing to do now was wait, see if Kira brought it up again or seemed to need to talk about it. If that happened, Corrine would try to think of something clear and honest to say about the situation, something her daughter could understand.

In the meantime, she felt like a lousy mother on top of everything else, like she'd dangled a carrot of family togetherness in front of her child and then snatched it away—which, come to think of it, was pretty much what she *had* done.

"Tomorrow is fine," Aleta said when Corrine called her that afternoon. "But doesn't Kira have dance classes?"

"She can skip, just this once."

"Well, all right. Shall I just pick her up at school and bring her with me?"

"Perfect."

"Anything else I can bring?"

"Orange nut bread?"

"As a matter of fact, I baked six loaves this morning—with cranberries this time, in honor of the season."

"Yum. Bring two."

Aleta promised she would.

Friday morning, after Corrine dropped Kira off at school, she went back home and got the tree and the decorations down from the attic. She put the tree together in its usual place of honor in the living room, front and center at the picture window. Last year, she'd bought a new one, with a thousand white lights and little clusters of pine cones tucked here and there among the branches. She arranged the green and red velvet tree skirt around the base, thinking how her grandmother, who'd died before Corrine was born, had made it when her mom, Kathleen, was a little girl.

Corrine set out the boxes of ornaments, so many handmade—some by her mother as a child, and then by Corrine. And now, last year and the year before that by Kira's small, clever hands. She ran the blinds up and left the tree lights on when she went into the kitchen to pop corn for stringing and heat up the spiced apple juice.

Kira came in shouting, "Mommy, the tree! The tree's in the window!"

Corrine poured the fluffy kernels of popped corn into the big red bowl that had been her mom's before it was hers and turned as her daughter burst into the kitchen. "It's pretty, isn't it, baby—even without the decorations?"

"It's *beautiful*."

Aleta appeared in Kira's wake, still wearing her coat and carrying the promised loaves of cranberry-orange bread. "Looks like everything's ready to go."

Kira jumped around, spinning in happy circles, literally dancing with excitement. "Are we doing it now, Mom? Are we decorating?"

"Oh, yes, we are." Corrine took the offered loaves from Aleta with a grateful smile. "Go with Grandma and hang up your coats. And then we'll get started—and Aleta, would you put on some Christmas music? I left a stack of CDs on the mantel."

"Will do," Aleta promised, unbuttoning her coat and herding Kira back out to the coatrack by the front door.

They worked for three hours, eating more popcorn than ever got strung; drinking hot cider; exclaiming over beloved, remembered ornaments to the accompaniment of six discs full of Christmas favorites. It was a beautiful, all-girls afternoon, one that a woman remembers for all her days.

Kira, pink-cheeked and beaming, sang along with "Silent Night" as she looped the red-and-green paper chain she'd made herself across the branches. They hung the stockings on the mantel, including the one for Corrine's mom. Corrine hadn't the heart to stop hanging Kathleen's stocking, even though this would be the third Christmas since her death.

"Do they have stockings in heaven?" Kira wondered.

"There are mysteries to which we never find the answer," Aleta said. "It's one of the very best things about life."

Kira looked puzzled. It was the expression she wore when she had no clue what the grownups were talking about. And then she burst into a bright smile. "Well, Granny Kate has a stocking at our house," she declared. "Even if she doesn't get one up there in heaven."

Corrine touched her daughter's shining blond head and wondered how much her child really remembered of Kathleen Lonnigan. Probably very little. She'd been so young when Kathleen died.

Kira ducked from under her touch, headed for the almost-empty popcorn bowl. Corrine glanced over to see Aleta watching. They shared a fond look and Corrine said a little prayer of gratitude to have Aleta now that her mom was gone.

The shared glance with Matt's mom brought Matt to mind. It stirred that aching in her heart that came too often the past few days. All those years, she'd refused to acknowledge that she cared for him as more than a friend or a lover. So much more. That she was *in* love with him. The denial of her true feelings had been a form of self-preservation, she saw now. It had worked really well, too. She wished she could go back to not understanding her own heart. Life was so much easier when you had certain necessary lies in place.

By four-thirty, Kira was starting to droop. Corrine and Aleta began arranging the manger scene on the mantel, setting the small plaster figures just so. Long ago, Corrine's mom had bought the figures—Mary, Joseph, the ox, the lamb, the shepherd boy, the three Kings, and baby Jesus in his bed of straw—one a year until she had them all.

Aleta tapped her shoulder and then raised a finger to her lips.

Corrine turned. Kira lay on the couch, her little hands tucked under her chin, her knees drawn up, conked out. Quietly, so as not to wake her, Aleta settled the afghan over her.

They finished setting up the crèche and then tiptoed to the kitchen, where Corrine swung the door to the hallway shut. She put the teakettle on. Aleta cut the cranberry-orange bread. They sat down to enjoy the snack.

Corrine stirred honey into her tea. "I…need to talk to you about Sunday."

"What?" Aleta sipped. And then she frowned. "Oh, no. You can't make it?"

"No, I can't. I'm gonna have to pass."

Aleta set down her cup with care. "I've been so looking forward to having you with us this year. And it won't be the same without Kira. She's such a joy. Matt never mentioned you all weren't coming."

Corrine stirred her tea some more, although the honey was already dissolved. "Um. Matt and Kira will be there, I'm sure."

Aleta's expression turned sad as she got the picture. She asked gently, "There's a problem?"

Corrine gave a shrug. "It's just not working out with Matt and me."

"Oh, no."

"Yeah. 'Fraid so."

Aleta reached across the table. Corrine reached, too. They clasped hands and shared a loving glance before letting go.

Matt's mom said, "If you need to talk about it, I'm always here to listen."

"Oh, I…no. I don't think so. Not now. But thank you."

"Any time. Just give me a call. Whatever you say will be kept strictly in confidence, I promise you—even from Davis. Yes, we tell each other everything. But I can make an exception for something like this. Believe me, he would understand."

Corrine wasn't so sure about that. But it didn't matter if Davis would understand or not because she wasn't saying anything about any of it. It just wasn't right, to go whining about Matt to his mom. "I do appreciate it, that you would offer…"

"It's open-ended. Remember. Any time, if you need me. You just give me a call."

"I know. And I'm so grateful. And about Christmas day…"

"Wait." Aleta's cup clinked sharply as she set it in the saucer. "Please. Christmas is almost two weeks away. Don't decide now—in fact, just be there if you want to be, on Christmas day. The door is always open for you, Corrine."

"Oh, but I—"

"Don't say anymore. There's no problem. You're one of the family. And that means you're always welcome at Bravo Ridge."

Corrine dreaded Saturday morning. But that didn't stop the day from coming. She had it firmly in her mind just how she would handle herself when she dropped Kira off. She would be polite and distant, do what was required of her and then get the heck out of there.

It worked out exactly as she planned it. She rang the bell. He opened the door.

"Daddy, I'm here!" Kira warbled.

"Hi," he said, looking over their daughter's head, his gaze on Corrine, unsmiling.

"Hi," Corrine answered.

Kira went in, already babbling about what a good time she'd had the day before. "Gramma came to our house to decorate the Christmas tree. We had so much fun!"

"'Bye." He shut the door.

And Corrine was left standing by herself on his wide front porch, bereft, her heart numb in her chest. She blinked, hard, to wipe the image of him, in old sweats and a worn-out college T-shirt, from her mind.

Then she turned, stiffly, and went down the steps to her waiting car.

Sunday night, when he brought Kira home to her, Corrine made herself stay in the living room. She called "Come in!" just like always when he rang the bell.

But really, it was nothing like always. He came in, he carried Kira up the stairs, he went back out. They didn't share so much as a glance. Corrine heard the door click shut as he left.

And for some sad reason, she thought of his dad— of the parallels between her and Matt and Aleta and Davis. Aleta had left Davis because she doubted his love. And Davis Bravo went after her. Corrine had to hand it to him. Davis never gave up until Aleta took him back, until she was totally convinced he did love her absolutely, without reservations. Until she had no doubt she was the woman for him.

Unlike his son. Who turned and walked away at the first hint of rejection.

Corrine almost smiled. Well, okay. She'd given Matt more than a hint. And *he* hadn't walked away, she had.

But still. When it came to love and passion and never giving up, Davis had Matt beat, hands down.

Then again…

Well, okay. She was lying to herself and she knew it. Davis had actually betrayed his wife. He damn well better have gone after her and bent over backward proving to her that he loved her to distraction and he knew he'd done wrong and would never, ever do such a thing again.

Matt hadn't betrayed anyone. He simply…hadn't loved her. Not in the way she wanted to be loved.

* * *

Monday, while Kira was at school and dance classes, Corrine went Christmas shopping. Everywhere she turned, there were Christmas carols playing and bright decorations. At home, her living room was a winter wonderland. Christmas would be there before she knew it. Friday was the annual invitation-only Christmas party at the Rose.

But before that, she needed to get through the anniversary of her mother's death. It had happened a week and a day before Christmas. On that day two years before Kathleen Lonnigan's car had been broadsided by a drunk driver as she drove home from North Star Mall with a trunk full of Christmas gifts.

Corrine hated that day. Nobody's mother should die eight days before Christmas. It made the joy of the season a little less so somehow. Corrine knew, realistically, that every year the pain would diminish. But it would never completely fade. Always, for the rest of her life, the holidays would include a certain grief, a certain sorrow. She missed her mom the most at this time of year.

I'm always with you, baby—there, in your heart. Never forget that I love you, that you're my beautiful, special girl.

"I know, Mom. But damn it, I still miss you. I always will."

The dreaded day came. Aleta called that morning and invited her to lunch. Corrine went. They ate at a place on the River Walk. Corrine felt the spirit of her mother, so close, smiling down on them. They talked of nothing important. It was just what Corrine needed on such a tough day.

The phone rang at five, as she was dishing up Kira's dinner.

She snagged the cordless off the counter and put it to her ear. "Hello."

"How you holding up?" *Matt.*

Her heart lurched to her throat and got stuck there. She swallowed, frantically, to make it drop back into her chest where it belonged. "I'm okay. It's, um, hard."

"Just checking on you."

It meant so much. Everything. That he remembered the worst day, the day she needed a friend. That no matter what happened between them as a man and a woman, he would always care, would always be there. She told herself she would focus on that and try to stop wanting to beat the crap out of him for not loving her enough, not loving her in the way that she wanted him to. "Thank you. Truly."

"No problem. Call if you need anything."

What if I need *you?* "I will. You want to talk to Kira?"

"Nah. Tell her that her daddy loves her and I'll see her on Saturday."

A click. And he was gone. She wanted to shout, No! You can't go. I have so much to say to you....

But she only gave Kira Matt's message and then got the food on the table.

That night at the Rose was a living hell. What was it about the holidays? It brought out the crazies.

Little Joe and his two-man crew had a busy night escorting a chain of drunken fools to the door. Four fights broke out—topping the Black Friday record of the month before. Corrine had a bottle of beer poured on her head by some SOB who didn't think she'd served him fast enough.

And it wasn't even the weekend yet.

She was never so glad to lock up and go home as she was that night. Plus, by then it was technically Thursday. Once again, she'd gotten past the dreaded day of the year when her mom died.

Thursday night was better. Only one fight. And she made it through her whole shift without anyone pouring beer in her hair.

By the time she got home in the wee hours of Friday morning, she was telling herself that Friday night would be even better. After all, it was the holiday party and you could only get in if you had one of those specially made invitations Lauren Evans had sent out. Because everyone Corrine invited was reasonably sane and not prone to drunken brawling, it was usually much more fun, and not nearly as stressful, as other nights. All the bartenders wore red and green in honor of the holiday and either Santa hats or cute cloth antlers.

Marilyn came early that night and Corrine went to work at six wearing red satin jeans and tooled suede boots to match. Her red cami was trimmed with faux white fur. When she got there, she slapped on a Santa hat, one with *nice* printed in glitter on the front—and *naughty* on the back.

By nine the place was packed. The band played good and loud, rock-and-roll versions of just about every Christmas song known to man. The crowd was getting frisky. All the regulars were calling for the girls to do what the Armadillo Rose bartenders were famous for—which was to get up and dance on the bar.

One by one, the girls got up and busted their favorite moves as everyone clapped and whooped and hollered. It was fun and the place was rocking. For the first time since she walked out on Matt, Corrine was feeling the spirit of the season. She sashayed from table to table, her drink tray held high and the furry white tassel at the end of her Santa hat swaying in rhythm to every beat of the music.

Her bartenders were having a ball. Once the last one finished her solo on the bar, she signaled the rest of them. They all got up there, in a line, and linked arms across each other's shoulders. Those women could dance. You couldn't work at the Rose if you didn't know how to dance. Their booted feet pounded the bar, keeping rhythm with the drummer in the band, in a dazzling combination of grapevines, kicks and tapping feet. As a finish, they did the cancan, kicking high, stomping hard.

And then, someone was yelling, "Corrine! Come on, Corrine! We want Corrine!"

The chant was picked up and all at once everyone was clapping, including her bartenders, calling her name.

"Cor-rine, Cor-rine, Cor-rine, Cor-rine!"

She thought about the baby growing inside her, about how, soon enough, she wouldn't be able to dance on the bar. Not for months and months.

And she rarely danced on the bar anymore anyway. Back when, she'd been one of the best. The regulars used to call her name nightly. But since she'd had Kira, she'd given it up, left it to the other girls—except for on special occasions.

"Cor-rine, Cor-rine, Cor-rine, Cor-rine!"

Well, all right. Why the hell not? If this wasn't a special occasion, what was? One last time. Because it was Christmas. Because she still could.

She handed her tray to a big guy with a bald head. And then she wove her way through the packed room to the bar. When she got there, she shouted, "Gimme a hand up, ladies!"

Everyone burst into catcalls and whistles and loud applause.

Corrine raised her arms. Eager hands reached down. She braced a foot on a bar stool and gave a push and she was up there. The line parted in the middle, the other girls moving sideways to give her some room.

The band launched into George Thorogood's "Rock n Roll Christmas."

And Corrine danced.

It was a fast, fun song. She laughed and threw her arms up in the air. She shimmied and shook and tapped her red boots, stomping furious rhythm with the fast, rocking beat, swinging her head from side to side, making her hair fly along with her Santa hat, really letting loose.

She heard shouts of encouragement. Everyone in the place was clapping in time. Loud whoops and whistles punctuated every move. Corrine danced on, lost in the joy of it, in the fun. In the freedom.

The best thing about dancing was how the world fell away. All her worries and cares, her hurts and her sadness. They were lost in the music, in the beauty of sound and her body's eager response to it.

She felt the last bars of the song approaching and turned to give the room her back, raising her arms high, shaking her hips for all she was worth, letting a shimmy slide through her, shoulders to toes. And then spinning, with a lift of one boot, arms high, around once and then again, stopping finally when she faced the room, throwing her arms wide and dropping into a low bow as the band hit that final note.

Breathless, she stood tall again, bowed again, smiling wide, accepting the wave of appreciative applause, the shouts of "Oh, yeah! That's the way you do it!" the whoops and whistles and excited, approving cries.

She pressed her hand to her heaving chest and held the other arm high, then dropped forward from the waist a third and final time.

And it was then, as she started to rise again, lifting her head and gazing out over the crowd, that she saw him.

Matt—right there, front and center, between a tall brunette and a hefty man with a red beard.

Matt. Oh, God. What was he doing here?

Yes, she always sent him an invitation. But it had never occurred to her that he might come. Not this year.

Not after last Sunday night.

Matt. He stared in her eyes. Heat flared. And it was six years ago, all over again. That first night she ever saw him, the night they made Kira.

The night that started it all.

Chapter Fourteen

No!

Corrine was *not* going there with him. Not tonight. Not ever again. She tore her gaze away from him.

Somehow, she'd ended up alone on the bar. She needed to fix that, and fast. She caught the eye of Lacy James, one of her bartenders, arguably the best among a crew of excellent dancers. Corrine gave her the signal—the slightest tip of her head.

Lacy knew the drill. With a loud, "Yahoo!" she jumped up beside Corrine and started to shimmy. Corrine gave the high sign. The band struck up the next tune.

Corrine jumped down onto the wooden slats on the business side of the bar. She clapped, her hands high, until the sound caught on and everyone was clapping and shouting encouragements at Lacy, who was knocking their socks off up there on the bar.

That gave Corrine the opening she needed. In seconds, she was under the flap of counter at the end of the bar and then slipping through the swinging door to the back room.

With the beat of the music pounding through the concrete floor under her boots she made for her office, where she could shut the door and lock it—and what?

Wait, she supposed. For what she wasn't exactly sure. Maybe for Matt to give up and leave.

She ducked into her office and swung the door shut— only it didn't quite close.

Because Matt had his hand out, stopping it. She'd thought she'd escaped him, but no such luck.

Fine. She flung the door wide, braced her hands on her hips. *"What?"*

He didn't say anything, only stepped forward and pushed the door shut behind him, trapping her in the room with him.

"Matt…"

He still didn't talk. What he did was reach for her and pull her into his strong arms. She should have resisted, she knew that. He had no call to hold her. Not now. Not ever again.

But the feel of him—the scent of him—so beloved, so well-remembered. It was too much for her—*he* was too much for her. His nearness, his touch…it all made her weak. She clung to him, sighing, lifting her mouth for the kiss he offered, a kiss of equal parts heat and aching tenderness.

When he lifted his head, he said, "I do love you, Corrie. You're everything to me."

And then he let go of her.

And as soon as he let go, he turned and left her.

She stared at the empty doorway where he had been, raising her hand to touch her lips, where she still felt his kiss, the heat in it. The longing.

It began to seem possible that she had misjudged him.

The next day was Saturday. She took Kira to him.

He was polite. Reserved, even.

She could almost wonder if that kiss the night before had really happened. If those words he'd said were only in her mind, a delusion of her yearning, aching heart.

"See you Sunday night," he said, as she turned to go.

"All right, then."

And he shut the door.

Sunday night was the usual. He rang the bell, she called, "Come in!" He carried their sleeping daughter up the stairs.

The only difference came as he was leaving. He paused in the arch between the living room and the entry way.

"About Christmas this year…"

She made her lips form a smile. "Yeah?" As a rule, she had Kira Christmas Eve and Christmas morning. Matt would pick her up before noon and take her with him to the ranch for the gift exchange with his family and then the Bravo's Christmas dinner.

"We'll do it the same as always?"

Her heart sank. But she spoke in a friendly tone. "Yeah. Sure."

He rapped his knuckles on the inner wall of the arch. "Well. Guess that's it then." And he left.

She sat up late that night, wrapping presents, thinking about what he'd said to her Friday night at the Rose.

I do love you, Corrie. You're everything to me.

Those words meant a lot. Maybe he thought the ball was in her court now.

Maybe it was.

Although what she ought to do next, she wasn't quite sure. Yes, she was too proud. She knew that. She still felt she needed more from him than "I love you," however sincere he had sounded when he said it. But exactly what more did she want?

She couldn't say.

She didn't see or hear from Matt in the next couple of days.

And then suddenly it was Christmas Eve. The Rose would be closed until the twenty-sixth. She had all day, all evening and the next morning to be with her daughter, to enjoy the holiday as a family of two.

They shared a leisurely breakfast of Kira's favorite, French toast. Then she helped Kira wrap her gifts for Matt's family. They went to a movie at noon, had ice cream after and got back home at a little past three.

Corrine kissed Kira and told her to go on upstairs for her nap.

Kira drooped her shoulders and stuck out her cute little chin. "Mommy. It's Christmas. I don't need a nap…"

Corrine shook her head. "You're sleepy. You can hardly keep your eyes open."

Kira whined some more and then Corrine offered a compromise. She let Kira get her favorite blanket and rest on the couch, where she could see the Christmas tree—and where she fell asleep almost before Corrine finished tucking her blanket around her.

Corrine was turning for the kitchen when the doorbell rang. She hurried to answer, in hopes of avoiding a second ring and the chance that Kira would wake up again.

It was Davis Bravo, of all people. "Merry Christmas, Corrine."

"Uh. Well." What could he be after? It couldn't be good. "Merry Christmas to you, Davis."

"I wonder if I might have a word?"

A word. He wanted a *word* with her.

What word? Why? She remembered all the cruel things he had said to her in the past. She didn't need that. Not on Christmas Eve. Not ever.

She was about to say no but stopped herself. He'd treated her respectfully in recent years—and all the more so since Aleta had stayed with her while they were separated. It hardly made sense that he would want to give her a hard time now.

And then she remembered Tabby Ellison's threats. Was this about Tabby, then?

"Corrine?" he asked, looking a little bit nervous. Maybe because she'd stood there trying to figure out what he was up to while staring blankly in his direction for the last couple of minutes.

She stirred herself to action, stepping back, whispering, "Kira's asleep on the couch. Let's go to the kitchen."

Once in there, she closed the door and offered coffee. He waved it away and took a seat at the table. "I'll get right to it," he said.

"Please do." She folded her arms protectively across her middle and leaned against the counter.

"We missed you at the ranch Sunday before last."

She frowned and then remembered. "Oh, the day you all decorated the tree…"

He gave a regal nod of his silver head. "I know that Aleta invited you. She was so pleased you were coming. And then you didn't show up. She was downright evasive when I asked her why not."

Corrine didn't beat around the bush. "Matt and I are on the outs. She was respecting my privacy, I imagine, by not discussing me with you."

He grunted. "Don't try to tell me that you don't love him."

His frankness surprised her. But all right. If he wanted to play it straight, she could handle that. She shrugged. "The problem was more that I didn't believe he loves me."

"'Didn't.' Past tense. I'll take that to mean you're finally seeing the light."

"Um. The light?"

"My son's in love with you. You don't have to worry about that. You never did."

She blinked. "I didn't?"

Davis actually chuckled. "How is it that you young people put it? You rocked his world. You always have. He was afraid of that at first. You can't blame a man for exercising a little caution. Especially a man like Matt, who had his life all mapped out until you came along and changed everything."

Corrine whirled around, grabbed a glass, ran water in it and drank it down. She plunked it on the counter and turned back to Matt's dad. "Sorry. It's hard for me to believe that we're having this conversation."

"Simply put, I'm here to apologize. I treated you like crap. I needed a lesson in humility. Recently, I got it. And when my life went to hell and Aleta left me, you were there. You took her in. She needed a home away from home and you gave her the space she needed. And then you let me join her in it. I owe you a lot. You gave me the chance to win my wife back."

She was getting kind of choked up. She waved a hand. "Hey. My pleasure."

A wry smile curved his mouth. "You're going to forgive me, then?"

"Hell. It's Christmas. Why not?"

Davis Bravo threw back his head and laughed. "You're a spunky gal, Corrine."

"Gee, thanks. I think."

"Give Matt a break, will you?"

"I'm considering it."

"Good. Come to Christmas at the ranch tomorrow."

"I'm considering that, too."

He pushed back the chair and stood. "One more thing."

"Yeah?"

"Yesterday, I had a visitor at the office…"

She'd known that was coming. "Let me guess. Tabby Ellison."

He nodded. "She had some crazy expectation that

I was going to make Matt call it off with you. I set her straight."

"How?"

"With the truth. I told her you not only have his child, you have his heart. And you always will. I told her to give it up and leave Matt alone. I said that continuing to chase after him would get her nowhere and also cause her unnecessary pain and humiliation."

"You're serious. You said all that?"

"I did."

"What did she do?"

"She ran out crying. And I called her father. I explained the situation. Rockford Ellison is a supremely practical man. He promised he would have a long talk with his daughter. I honestly don't believe that Tabitha will be bothering you again."

For Corrine, the rest of the day felt brighter somehow. Yes, she and Matt were still apart. She was seeing that she needed to do something about that.

But it was huge for her, that Davis had actually knocked on her door and asked her personally to come to Christmas at Bravo Ridge. That he had apologized for all the rotten things he'd said in the past. That he had stood up for her against Tabby Ellison. And even that he'd called her a "spunky gal." More than the corny, old-fashioned words, it was the *way* he had said it: "You're a spunky gal, Corrine." With respect. And real affection.

She and Kira had pizza for dinner. It was a family tradition started by Corrine's mom way back when Corrine was Kira's age. They had pizza and Pepsi in front of the TV while they watched "Home Alone." After the movie, she and Kira played Old Maid to the accompaniment of carols on the CD player.

At about nine, Kira yawned widely. "Mommy. It's past my bedtime."

"I thought, since it's a special night, that you could stay up as long as you wanted."

"You did?" Blue eyes widened at the wonder of that.

Corrine nodded. "I think you should take your bath, though. And put on your pjs…"

Kira didn't argue. She bounced up the stairs. Corrine followed her up and filled the tub for her, then went back downstairs to change the CD.

Twenty minutes later, she went back up, just to check. She found her daughter sound asleep across a still-made bed, wearing her pajamas. She'd gotten all ready for bed and then just crawled up there and conked out. Corrine put a blanket over her, turned off the light and tiptoed from the room, pulling the door silently shut behind her.

Downstairs, she switched off the music and turned the lights down low, so the tree shone all the brighter. She kicked off her shoes and sat on the couch. Grabbing the afghan, she swung her legs up and wrapped the blanket around them.

She stared at the tree, admiring its beauty, appreciating the moment, letting herself kind of drift on a cloud of peace and good feelings, letting all her cares and worries fade….

The chime of the doorbell jolted her awake. She sat

up and raked her hair back off her forehead, blinking blearily at the mantel clock beside the manger scene she and Aleta had so lovingly arranged.

It was 1:00 a.m. Christmas morning. And there was someone at her door. She got up to answer.

But when she reached the entry hall, indecision took over. At one in the morning it could be anyone. Bad guys didn't always take Christmas off.

The phone rang. She went back to the living room to grab the cordless. "Hello?"

"You're awake." It was Matt.

"I am now." She clutched the phone tight. Could this be the Christmas present she wanted most of all? "Someone just rang my doorbell. Can you believe that?"

"So why don't you answer?"

She carried the phone back into the entry hall. "I was kind of worried it might be a burglar."

"On Christmas?"

"Well," she said, "you never know."

"Not a very good burglar, if he's ringing the doorbell."

"Hmm. Good point." Her door had a mail slot. As she watched, a white envelope appeared and slid to the floor. "Can you believe someone just sent me a letter?"

"Why don't you read it?"

"Think I should?"

"I *know* you should."

"Hold on."

"I'm right here," he told her. "I'm here and I'm not going anywhere."

Her hands were shaking. It was the craziest thing. "I think I have to put the phone down."

"Go ahead. I'll wait."

By then, she had her back to the wall, kind of bracing herself against it. With the phone in one hand and the letter in the other, she let her knees buckle. She slid down the wall until her butt met the floor. And then, with great care, she set the phone down beside her.

That left both hands free to deal with the envelope. Fumbling, the paper crackling as her fingers shook, she managed to get it open and slide the letter inside free.

It was one page, printed off a computer. Single spaced.

It had a title, all in caps: *17 THINGS I LOVE ABOUT YOU.*

And centered, below that, ...*And Can't Live Without (in no particular order).*

A list. He'd written a list! It was so like him.

She started reading, her heart so full she marveled it could hold all the love within it, her tears rising, pooling, streaming unashamed down her cheeks.

1. The way you look in the morning with no makeup and that grouchy frown
2. The way you move when you're dancing
3. Because of the daughter you gave me
4. Because of the amazing job you're doing raising said daughter
5. Because of the new baby. I know he or she will have the best mother there is
6. The simple fact that you happen to be the most beautiful woman in the world
7. Another fact: If not for you, I would still be a

spoiled, selfish, stick-up-the-ass rich boy without a
clue of all that I was missing

8. Because you work hard and are perfectly capable of
   taking care of yourself
9. Because you tell the truth
10. Because of your mind. It's a beautiful mind
11. Because you'll do anything for a friend
12. And speaking of that, because you took care of my
    mom when she needed it—in the *way* that she
    needed it
13. Because you have a sense of humor. In the long run,
    a guy really needs a woman with one of those
14. Because the first time I saw you naked, I thought
    I would die
15. And every other time since
16. Because you never take any crap from me—or
    anyone else for that matter
17. Because you are my beacon. Of sanity. Of truth

P.S.—Please take me back. I can live without
marriage if that's how you want it, but don't make
me live without you in my arms at night, across
the table from me in the morning and beside me,
in the good times and the tough times, too.

"Corrie?" His voice, from the phone on one side,
through the door on the other. "Corrie, you still there?"

She swiped the streaming tears away, grabbed the
phone and stuck it in a pocket as she shoved herself back
up the wall to her feet. Once there, she turned to the door.

He stood on the other side, his eyes full of hope, a

giant poinsettia held in his hands. Shyly, he told her, "I thought flowers, you know? But then I saw this…"

She grabbed his arm and hauled him inside, shoving the door shut. "Thank you." She took the plant from him, set it on the narrow entry hall table. And then she reached for him.

He gathered her into his arms. "You cried…"

"Yeah."

He bent, kissed one wet cheek and then the other. "I love you. So much. I don't know why I never said it. It was only…I had a plan for my life. It was all laid out in my mind, just how it would go—college, my masters, home to work at BravoCorp…"

"And get richer than you already were."

He nodded. "And I always did plan to get married—but not till my mid-thirties."

"…to a woman who would never own a bar—let alone get up and dance on one."

"And then I met you."

"The wrong woman at the wrong time."

"…who actually happened to be so damn right. I let my rigid plans ruin our chance at love and happiness."

She slipped her arms around his waist, kissed that manly cleft in his chin. "But see, Matt, that's the thing about love. When there's love, there can be a second chance."

"You mean that?" Hope shone in his beautiful eyes.

"Oh, yes. I was too proud. I'll work on that. You still got that ring you bought me?"

"Corrie." His voice held reverence. And surprise. "You're serious?"

"Seventeen reasons, huh? I'm impressed."

"I've got the ring. At home. I didn't bring it. I was afraid you might think I was pushing…."

"Marry me, Matt."

"Say that again."

"Marry me."

"I thought you'd never ask."

In the morning, Kira came downstairs to find her parents kissing by the fireplace.

"Daddy!" She ran to him, her arms out wide.

He scooped her up. She hooked one small arm around his neck and reached for her mom with the other. When she had them both good and close, she announced, "Happy Christmas to our family." She planted one smacking kiss on Matt's cheek and then one on Corrine's.

And then instantly she was squirming to get down and get to the tree with all those presents under it.

After the gifts were opened, Corrine made pancakes. And after breakfast, she and Kira got dressed. Matt had only the clothes he'd arrived in the night before, so they went to his house, where he showered and changed. And gave Corrine her engagement ring.

And then they drove out to Bravo Ridge.

They parked in the big circle in front of the imposing white ranch house with its grand row of white pillars holding up the deep front verandah, each one wrapped in a spiral of greenery that sparkled with tiny lights. Aleta emerged through the front door as they mounted the wide steps.

Tears shone in her eyes at the sight of Corrine. "Welcome," she said. "I'm so glad you're here." And she held out her arms.

Corrine went first into her loving embrace. And then Kira and then Matt. After the hugs, Aleta herded them inside. Corrine crossed the threshold with wonder and joy in her heart.

It was a beautiful day. A magical day. A day that Corrine had never believed would come. It was her first Christmas at Bravo Ridge.

* * * * *

Watch for Caleb's story, VALENTINE BRIDE,
coming in February 2010,
only from Silhouette Special Edition.

* * *

'THIS EVENING I'm flying to New York for two weeks,'
Jasim imparted with a casualness that made her heart sink
like a stone. 'That's why I had you brought here. I own this
apartment and you'll be comfortable here while I'm abroad.'

'I can afford my own accommodation although I may not
need it for long. I'll have another job by the time you
get back—'

Jasim released a slightly harsh laugh. 'There's no need for
you to look for another position. How would I ever see you?
Don't you understand what I'm offering you?'

Elinor stood very still. 'No, I must be incredibly thick
because I haven't quite worked out yet what you're offering
me….'

His charismatic smile slashed his lean dark visage.
'Naturally, I want to take care of you….'

'No, thanks.' Elinor forced a smile and mentally willed him not to demean her with some sordid proposition. 'The only man who will ever take *care* of me with my agreement will be my husband. I'm willing to wait for you to come back but I'm not willing to be kept by you. I'm a very independent woman and what I give, I give freely.'

Jasim frowned. 'You make it all sound so serious.'

'What happened between us last night left pure chaos in its wake. Right now, I don't know whether I'm on my head or my heels. I'll stay for a while because I have nowhere else to go in the short term. So maybe it's good that you'll be away for a while.'

Jasim pulled out his wallet to extract a card. 'My private number,' he told her, presenting her with it as though it was a precious gift, which indeed it was. Many women would have done just about anything to gain access to that direct hotline to him, but his staff guarded his privacy with scrupulous care.

Before he could close the wallet, his blood ran cold in his veins. How could he have made such a serious oversight? What if he had got her pregnant? He knew that an unplanned pregnancy would engulf his life like an avalanche, crush his freedom and suffocate him. He barely stilled a shudder at the threat of such an outcome and thought how ironic it was that what his older brother had longed and prayed for to secure the line to the throne should strike Jasim as an absolute disaster....

* * *

What will proud Prince Jasim do if Elinor is expecting his royal baby? Perhaps an arranged marriage is the only solution! But will Elinor agree? Find out in DESERT PRINCE, BRIDE OF INNOCENCE by Lynne Graham [#2884], available from Harlequin Presents® in January 2010.

HPEX0110B

Bestselling Harlequin Presents author

Lynne Graham

brings you an exciting new miniseries:

PREGNANT BRIDES

Inexperienced and expecting, they're forced to marry

Collect them all:

DESERT PRINCE, BRIDE OF INNOCENCE

January 2010

RUTHLESS MAGNATE, CONVENIENT WIFE

February 2010

GREEK TYCOON, INEXPERIENCED MISTRESS

March 2010

www.eHarlequin.com

REQUEST YOUR FREE BOOKS!

2 FREE NOVELS PLUS 2 FREE GIFTS!

Silhouette®

SPECIAL EDITION®

Life, Love and Family!

YES! Please send me 2 FREE Silhouette Special Edition® novels and my 2 FREE gifts (gifts are worth about $10). After receiving them, if I don't wish to receive any more books, I can return the shipping statement marked "cancel." If I don't cancel, I will receive 6 brand-new novels every month and be billed just $4.24 per book in the U.S. or $4.99 per book in Canada. That's a savings of at least 15% off the cover price! It's quite a bargain! Shipping and handling is just 50¢ per book.* I understand that accepting the 2 free books and gifts places me under no obligation to buy anything. I can always return a shipment and cancel at any time. Even if I never buy another book from Silhouette, the two free books and gifts are mine to keep forever.

235 SDN EYN4 335 SDN EYPG

Name	(PLEASE PRINT)

Address	Apt. #

City	State/Prov.	Zip/Postal Code

Signature (if under 18, a parent or guardian must sign)

Mail to the **Silhouette Reader Service:**
IN U.S.A.: P.O. Box 1867, Buffalo, NY 14240-1867
IN CANADA: P.O. Box 609, Fort Erie, Ontario L2A 5X3

Not valid to current subscribers of Silhouette Special Edition books.

Want to try two free books from another line?
Call 1-800-873-8635 or visit www.morefreebooks.com.

* Terms and prices subject to change without notice. Prices do not include applicable taxes. Sales tax applicable in N.Y. Canadian residents will be charged applicable provincial taxes and GST. Offer not valid in Quebec. This offer is limited to one order per household. All orders subject to approval. Credit or debit balances in a customer's account(s) may be offset by any other outstanding balance owed by or to the customer. Please allow 4 to 6 weeks for delivery. Offer available while quantities last.

SSE09R

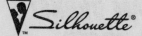
Silhouette®

COMING NEXT MONTH
Available December 29, 2009

SPECIAL EDITION

#2017 PRESCRIPTION FOR ROMANCE—Marie Ferrarella
The Baby Chase
Dr. Paul Armstrong had a funny feeling about Ramona Tate, the beautiful new PR manager for his famous fertility clinic. Was she a spy trying to uncover the institute's secrets…or a well-intentioned ingenue trying to steal his very heart?

#2018 BRANDED WITH HIS BABY—Stella Bagwell
Men of the West
Private nurse Maura Donovan had sworn off men—until she was trapped in close quarters during a freak thunderstorm with her patient's irresistible grandson Quint Cantrell. One thing led to another, and now she was pregnant with the rich rancher's baby!

#2019 LOVE AND THE SINGLE DAD—Susan Crosby
The McCoys of Chance City
On a rare visit to his hometown, photojournalist Donovan McCoy discovered he was the father of a young son. But the newly minted single dad wouldn't be single for long, if family law attorney—and former Chance City beauty queen—Laura Bannister had anything to say about it.

#2020 THE BACHELOR'S NORTHBRIDGE BRIDE—
Victoria Pade
Northbridge Nuptials
Prim redhead Kate Perry knew thrill seeker Ry Grayson spelled trouble. It was a case of the unstoppable bachelor colliding with the unmovable bachelorette. But did the undeniable attraction between them suggest there were some Northbridge Nuptials in their near future?

#2021 THE ENGAGEMENT PROJECT—Brenda Harlen
Brides & Babies
Gage Richmond was a love-'em-and-leave-'em type—until his CEO dad demanded he settle down or miss out on a promotion. Now it was time to see if beautiful research scientist Megan Rourke would pose as Gage's fake fiancée…and if their feelings would stay fake for long.

#2022 THE SHERIFF'S SECRET WIFE—Christyne Butler
*Bartender Racy Dillon didn't expect to run into her hometown nemesis, Sheriff Gage Steele, in Vegas—let alone marry him in a moment of abandon! Now they were headed back to their small town with a big secret…but was there more to this whiplash wedding than met the eye?

SSECNMBPA1209